W9-AVR-610

The Cannibals of Sunset Drive

The Cannibals of Sunset Drive

by Dan K. Carlsruh

Macmillan Publishing Company
New York

Maxwell Macmillan Canada
Toronto

Maxwell Macmillan International
New York   Oxford   Singapore   Sydney

12-94-143

Macmillan Publishing Company is part of the Maxwell
Communication Group of Companies.
Macmillan Publishing Company
866 Third Avenue
New York, NY 10022
Maxwell Macmillan Canada, Inc.
1200 Eglinton Avenue East
Suite 200
Don Mills, Ontario M3C 3N1
First edition
Printed in the United States of America

10 9 8 7 6 5 4 3 2 1

The text of this book is set in 12 point Bembo.

Library of Congress Cataloging-in-Publication Data
Carlsruh, Dan K.
    The cannibals of Sunset Drive / by Dan K. Carlsruh. — 1st ed.
    p.   cm.
    Summary: Ten-year-old Mike is convinced that the old monastery in
his town is inhabited by a group of cannibal monks, until he meets the
sole occupant of the building.
    ISBN 0-02-717110-8
    [1. Fear—Fiction. 2. Friendship—Fiction. 3. Monks—Fiction. 4.
Christmas—Fiction.] I. Title.
PZ7.C21683Can 1993 [Fic]—dc20 92-40568

This story is dedicated to
Eve
Esther
Rachel
Abe
Sam
and Kate
and to memories of Moon Lake
and Marshmallow mountains

1
The Tower

They're watching me.

They see everything I do. They watch as I take off my pants and throw them over the chair. They see me pull my pajamas out of the drawer and put them on.

They sit in the tower and watch me with their red, glowing eyes.

Pulling the shades down over the window wouldn't help. They would still see every move I make. Cannibals can see right through things like walls and curtains.

I turn on my night-light and dive under my blanket. They must be disappointed. They can't get me as long as my light is on and I'm under the blanket.

They'll have to wait for another night when I'm not so careful. Maybe by now they realize that I'm too smart to turn off my light and sleep on top of my blanket. Maybe they're watching Kenny up on Sagebrush Avenue, or Pratt down the road instead.

Without my night-light I have little protection. One night last month a big storm swung the trees outside, and the lights suddenly went off. I threw the covers over my head and ran out of my room, across the hall, and into Mom and Dad's room. I jumped onto the bottom of their bed and curled up in a ball under my blanket.

Dad just laughed.

"Mike?" Mom asked. "Are you all right?"

"I'm okay," I yelled from under my blanket.

"He looks like a turtle." Dad laughed even harder.

How could he laugh when my very life was in danger? The lights were off and my only protection was the blanket, and all he could do was laugh. Would he laugh when the cannibal bats carried me away to the tower?

Would he still be laughing when they returned my bones in a small plastic bag with a thank-you note inside?

> Dear Mike's Dad:
> Thank you for Mike. He was delicious!
> Sincerely,
> The Cannibal Monks

I survived that night, but only because I was thinking fast. Each night is a new battle between me and the cannibal monks.

I peek out from under my blanket. Through my window I can see the tower rise up from the center of the vampire-cannibal castle on the hill. It even rises above the large oak trees that surround the castle. I bet from the top of the tower they can even see some of the kids who live in the city five miles away. But they are more interested in the kids in our neighborhood, especially the boys.

Pratt says they like young boy meat the best. They look at us as if we were juicy steaks on the grill.

The castle is almost a half mile away, but the moon shines down on it and makes it look like it's in my backyard. And it might as well be. Everyone knows that cannibals have telescopic eyes.

Dad says the tower is just a part of the monastery. He says a bell probably used to be in the tower. But none of my friends ever remember any music coming from the tower. We've only seen red, glaring eyes looking over the neighborhood. Looking for their next meal.

The castle, or monastery as Dad calls it, takes up a whole block on Sunset Drive. Sunset Drive is the highest road in the whole neighborhood. Dad says that all the snobs live on Sunset. He says that snobs like to build homes higher than anybody else so that they can look down on everybody.

Kimberly Hansen lives on Sunset Drive. She's a snob. Pratt says that Kimberly's mom and dad buy an entire toy store for Christmas and let her play in it.

The homes on Sunset Drive aren't newer than all the other homes. They were built at the same time as the rest of the houses in the neighborhood. But they are much bigger and have nicer cars.

But next to all the fancy cars and big homes is the ancient rock castle with its evil tower. A thick stone wall surrounds the entire monastery. It's old and eerie. . . . It doesn't belong here.

Mom says the monastery was built almost a hundred years ago. But she's wrong. Pratt says it's at least a thousand years old. He says his brother told him it was built by an evil tribe of Indians. Pratt's brother should know. He's in high school.

Dad says the monastery used to own all of the land where the neighborhood is built. He says the monks from the monastery used to farm wheat, corn, and hay.

Monks are supposed to be like preachers, but they don't preach. They just live together with other monks and do a lot of praying.

But no one has ever seen the monks. That's because they are all in the tower looking down at the young boys in the neighborhood and seeing how well we are fattening up.

And they only come out at night. Everyone knows that sunlight can boil the skin off of a vampire. And cannibal monks are like cousins to vampires. They can even turn into bats and fly around. They look for boys who turn off their lights and sleep on top of their blankets.

No one has ever seen a light in the monastery. Mom says that's because they go to sleep very early. Mom doesn't know. It's because cannibals don't want their skin to boil and evaporate.

Pratt, Kenny, and I are now the prime age in the neighborhood. Pratt says that ten is the best age for boy meat. He said it's a known fact that ten-year-old boys have the worst survival rate of any age in this neighborhood. The monks will eat an adult, or even a girl, for the fiber. But they still prefer ten-year-old boys.

In three months I'll be eleven, and will not be the cannibals' favorite meal. I may not be totally safe from them as long as I live in this neighborhood, but at least I won't be their favorite dish.

The graves in the monastery's garden remind us of the fate of other ten-year-old boys. Twelve nicely made graves are the final resting places of the delicious, tender meals. Or at least of what's left of them. And the last thing any of us wants to be is number thirteen.

It's not fair that I have a window that can be seen from the tower. Why are Dad and Mom helping these monsters? They should know better. But every time I explain to Dad, he just rolls his eyes in his head and tells me to quit watching scary movies on TV.

So they've left me to survive on my own. If I can just make it until I'm eleven. Mom's always telling me to make plans early in my life so that I can work toward them. Plans like what I want to be when I grow up.

All I really want to be when I grow up is alive.

2

The Wall

Faster! Faster!

My legs hurt and my lungs feel like they're going to burst out my side and fall to the ground.

Faster! Faster!

I look down to my feet, trying to forget the pain. My red-and-white tennis shoes make a pink blur as I pedal down Rosewood Lane. The pain in my side wants to quit, but I have to keep going. If I don't, I will have to walk the wall.

Faster! Faster!

I take a quick glance behind me to make sure that Kenny is still there. Good, he's a few feet in back. With Kenny safely behind me, I can concentrate on Pratt, who is only a few feet in front.

Pratt always wins. He's the fastest bike rider in the neighborhood. I may not beat Pratt, but at least I'll take second place, and second place is a nice place to be.

Last place is the worst. Last-place finishers have to walk the wall.

I turn up Ash Street. It's a steep hill up to Sunset. I

glance back again to Kenny. He pedals like he's racing for his life. I don't blame him. This may be the last bike ride of his life. If he loses, it's the wall.

Faster! Faster!

As the road gets steeper, I put my head down and stand on my pedals. I'll take second place if it kills me. Better to die out here than behind the wall. My head aches, my legs feel like cement. My lungs feel burned. I want to throw up.

Pratt makes it to the top first. He raises his arms in victory and turns around to see how the battle between me and Kenny is going.

I'm too tired to look behind me, but I can't hear Kenny breathing. He must have fallen back.

I make it! Second place. I haven't been in last place ever since Dad gave me my lucky coin. It's an old 1954 fifty-cent piece with Ben Franklin on the front and the Liberty Bell on the back.

I pull over to the curb, jump off my bike, and collapse on the grass. My lungs take in large gulps of air. It hurts as my chest heaves up and down.

No wall today. I can live until the next race. I reach into my pocket and pull out my coin. I rub Ben's face with my fingers, flip the coin into the air, and put it back into my pocket.

"Hey, Mike, look at Kenny," Pratt says, pointing down the hill.

I roll over and see Kenny sprawled out on the grass halfway down Ash. I had nothing to worry about. He had given up long before the top and stopped by the fire hydrant.

"Hey, Kenny!" Pratt yells. "You better get your walking shoes on!"

Kenny groans. I'm sure he's thinking up some excuse. Kenny's always finding excuses.

I sit up and look at Pratt. He doesn't seem tired at all. He beats us in everything but never gets tired. My dad says he's a "natural."

"You think he can make it without falling?" I say, looking at Kenny.

"Hope so. If he falls in, I'm not going in after him."

"Me neither."

I shudder at the thought of Kenny falling off the wall and into the garden. It would probably be the last time we saw him—alive at least.

"We better get started," Pratt says as he rides down toward Kenny. "The sun's going down."

There's probably only an hour of sunlight left. Without the sun, Kenny has no chance on the wall. Only the sun keeps the monastery cannibals in their dark, gloomy rock castle.

Pratt once said he saw the cannibals looking out the windows, waiting for a young boy to fall into the garden. Then they would wait for the sun to go down so that they could get the trapped boy.

I stand up and walk over to my bike. My legs complain with each step. They feel heavy, like all the blood in my body has fallen down to my feet. I get onto my bike and ride down to Kenny and Pratt.

Kenny is still lying on the grass, looking pale and sick.

"You okay?" I ask.

"I don't feel too good," he moans.

"You try to get out of this, and I'll tell Jenny that you're a chicken," Pratt warns.

Kenny groans louder. He would rather have his bike stolen than have Jenny know he was a chicken. Jenny Wilson is the best thing a boy in fifth grade can look at. And a girl as nice as Jenny surely wouldn't like a chicken.

Kenny rolls over and gets up slowly. He brushes off his pants and looks at the orange sun.

"But it's almost dark!"

Pratt reaches over and pulls up Kenny's bike. "We got time if you hurry."

Kenny reluctantly gets onto his bike. "I bet they don't have to wait until the sun's all the way down before they come out."

"Course they do," I remind Kenny. "Anybody knows that if a cannibal walks out with even a ray of sunlight, his skin will boil and evaporate."

"How do you know?" Kenny protests.

"Just do."

He doesn't argue. He knows he's going to walk the wall, light or no light. Arguing about it will just take more time, more precious sunlight.

"Let's go," Pratt says as he starts off toward Sunset Drive.

I follow behind Pratt while Kenny reluctantly follows both of us.

We finally get up to the tall rock wall of the monastery. Only a small portion of the sun is still above the horizon. Kenny better hurry.

The wall makes a huge square. In the center of the square is the monastery and tower. The monastery is just one big building. Between the wall and the monastery are grass and giant oak trees.

The front part of the monastery is a courtyard with lawn, bushes, and trees. An iron gate comes in from Sunset Drive and goes into this courtyard. This is the only break in the entire wall. The gate is rusted and probably hasn't been opened for hundreds of years. There's no need for it to open, though. Cannibal-vampire monks can fly with their bat wings at night.

A stone path goes from the iron gate to a large wooden door. The door goes into the monastery.

At the back is the garden and the graves.

We get off our bikes and walk up to the wall. The setting sun makes the wall glow orange.

"Climb on," Pratt says to Kenny.

"Give me a minute," Kenny says nervously.

He looks up the wall, hoping he can make it alive. He knows somebody at school who knew somebody named George who fell off the wall into the garden, never to be seen again. George is probably number twelve, the last of the graves in the garden.

The garden on the other side of the wall is full of white daisies, oak trees, and large red roses that poke their heads above the wall.

"Blood makes the roses so red," Pratt once told us. "And the dead bodies buried in the garden make the trees grow so tall."

Pratt was right. The twelve graves are just at the other end of the garden, all nicely marked with small white markers. Some of the markers are made of stone, some with wood. Next to the graves is a small wooden shed. Pratt says that's where the monks prepare what's left of their dinner for burial.

Kenny's dad said the graves are where some of the monks from the monastery are buried.

But Kenny's dad doesn't know. Cannibals never die, at least as long as they have young boys to feed on. The graves are the remains of boy pizza and boy stew.

"Come on, Kenny," I say bravely, knowing I get to stay down on the ground. "There's only a few minutes of sun left."

"Awright, awright!" Kenny says.

He takes a deep breath, closes his eyes for a moment, then looks up the wall.

"I'm ready."

I guess Kenny's as calm as can be expected. This isn't the first time he's had to climb the wall, so he knows he has a chance. But the last time, he almost fell into the garden. He says one of the roses sticking up over the wall grabbed his ankle and tried to pull him in. He jumped off to the ground just in time. He sprained his ankle, but at least he was alive.

Now he has to try it again.

The loser only has to walk the back part of the wall,

the part above the garden. The part next to the twelve graves.

Kenny puts his hands onto the wall, feeling for places where he can hang on. He pulls himself up and slowly reaches for another handhold. The wall is almost ten feet high, and it takes a while to get to the top.

He finally reaches the top and pulls himself up, lying belly-down on the wall. He steadies himself for a moment, then carefully stands up straight. His arms stretch out to balance him.

The top of the wall is as wide as a sidewalk, but when you're up that high, your knees begin to shake and you feel like you're on a tightrope. Not to mention the fact that if you fall into the garden, you become dinner for a gang of zombie boy-eaters.

Even though Pratt and I aren't climbing, our hearts beat faster and we hold our breaths. Kenny starts walking, looking only at his feet.

"Careful," Pratt yells.

What a stupid comment. Of course he's going to be careful. When you teeter between life and death, you're bound to be careful. It's like when Mom tells Dad to drive carefully. What does she think? That if she doesn't tell Dad to drive carefully, he's going to drive off the bridge?

"Careful," I yell up to Kenny.

Kenny doesn't pay any attention to us. He puts one foot a couple of inches in front of the other. It may be slow, but it's the best way to survive the wall.

Pratt and I walk along below Kenny. He's getting closer to the killer roses. A couple of them stick above the wall, waiting for fresh young boys to eat. Maybe they're sleeping now, so they won't grab for Kenny.

He stops just before he gets to the roses. He waits to see if the roses notice him. Perhaps the roses can remember the smell of Kenny, the young boy who got away.

After a few seconds of watching closely, Kenny moves on, a little faster this time. A pant leg brushes against one of the roses. Pratt and I gasp, hoping that he didn't wake them. The rose sleepily nods back down, unaware that a meal is passing it by.

Kenny gets bolder, or more scared, and walks faster. He looks like he's going to make it in record time. Pratt and I cheer him on from below.

Suddenly he stops. His arms and legs are frozen as he stares down into the garden.

"Just a few more feet," I encourage Kenny. "Come on, you can make it."

But he just stands there, barely breathing as he stares at something in the garden.

Pratt gives me a confused look. "You think the cannibals put a spell on him or something?"

Kenny suddenly dashes to the end of the wall and jumps off the edge, onto the grass. It wasn't even a sort-of run. It was a full-out sprint. And the jump wasn't any little hop. It was a G.I. Joe commando leap.

Kenny turns around and backs up like a crab. His eyes are wide and scared as he stares at the wall.

"Way to go!" Pratt yells as he runs over to Kenny. "You made that look like you were strolling down the sidewalk."

Except, of course, sidewalks don't try to eat boys.

Kenny stands up, still looking at the wall. He points to the wall, his hand shaking.

"There's another one," Kenny says in small gasps.

"Another what?" I ask.

"I saw it," Kenny says, looking at me like he saw the world's grossest movie. "It's another one."

Pratt grabs Kenny's arms and turns him around.

"Another what?"

Kenny looks sick. He takes a couple of deep breaths.

"There's thirteen."

My spine curdles in my backbone and my knees want to crumble to the ground. Pratt doesn't look like he's in the best shape, either.

When I see that Pratt is as scared as I am, I get even more scared. It takes a lot to scare Pratt. He can even go into his basement at night without closing his eyes or running up the stairs. If he's scared, there must be something to be really afraid of.

"You sure?" Pratt asks with a shaky voice.

Kenny backs up, mad and frightened. "There used to be twelve graves, right?"

"That's what there's always been," I say.

"Well, now there's thirteen."

My spine tingles again. There's something about the number thirteen that doesn't make me feel good.

"You counted wrong," Pratt says. He's feeling better

now that he's sure Kenny was just counting wrong.

"No sir," says Kenny. "It's off to the side of the others. It even has fresh dirt on top. Not even any grass."

I close my eyes, wishing I was behind the piano doing my lessons like I should be. Good boys do their lessons. They don't walk on the walls of cannibals and killer roses. And they definitely don't count graves.

"I don't believe it," Pratt says. "Let's look at them again."

"You crazy!" I scream. "Look at the sun. It won't be long before the cannibals come outside. If we climb that wall now, we could get our heads chopped off!"

"They didn't get Kenny when he was walking," Pratt says.

"Maybe it's a trap?" I say. "They made the grave so they could get our attention. I mean, if you're a cannibal, three heads are better than one."

"I'll tell Jenny. . . ."

"Tell her!" Kenny yells. "I'm getting out of here."

Kenny runs over to his bike, limping a bit on his resprained ankle. He gets onto his bike and races away, not even looking back at the wall.

I watch Kenny pedal as fast as he can down Sunset Drive toward home. I think that's the best idea and decide to follow.

"You coming?" Pratt asks.

I look back and see Pratt already climbing the wall. I want to say no and jump onto my bike, but my thrill side wants to climb the wall and count the graves.

It's the same thrill side of my brain that makes me

ride the triple loop at the parkway after eating four hot dogs, cotton candy, and a large order of onion rings.

It's the same thrill side that makes me peek through my fingers at a scary movie even after I covered my eyes.

I walk to the wall. My thrill side always wins.

The stones feel cold and wicked. The low sun now looks deep red. I start to climb.

As we get near the top, I slow down. I'm going to let Pratt put his head up first. If cannibals are waiting, maybe they'll just chop off Pratt's head and not wait for me to poke mine over the top.

Pratt gets to the top and looks over. His head doesn't come rolling off, so the cannibals must still be inside.

"Look at this," Pratt whispers.

I stick my head over and look down to where the graves are. In the corner are the usual twelve graves. But off to one side, under a blanket of freshly raked dirt, is number thirteen.

My thrill side wants to go home and do piano lessons.

Pratt starts to climb on top of the wall to get a better look. I can see all I want to from where I am.

Just as Pratt gets onto the wall, a bat darts out of the garden and past us. Pratt screams and jumps back down to the grass. Before I can figure out what's happening, I see Pratt riding his bike away from the monastery.

But I'm still hanging on to the wall, too scared to

move. I figure I better move slowly and act cool. Cannibals can smell fear.

As I slowly lower my head, a dark shadow moves by a window in the monastery!

I decide that slow isn't the best approach. I jump the rest of the way and hop onto my bike. I actually saw the figure of one of the monks walking inside. As far as I know, I'm the only one who has.

I don't even think about how tired my legs are as I race back down Sunset onto Ash. The sun is almost down, and it would be better if boys my age and with tender meat not be near the monastery when the last sun ray shines. Especially when the cannibal bats are already leaving the bell tower and smelling out new victims.

I'm pedaling so fast that I catch up to Pratt. At the bottom of Ash Street we turn onto Antelope Drive, the street where Pratt and I live.

Pratt reaches his home first. He's so scared that he jumps off his bike before it stops. He tumbles onto the ground but comes up running to his front door. The bike smashes into the garage door.

He runs inside and slams the door behind him. He's safe.

But I have two more blocks to go. I stand up on my pedals and move my feet as fast as they can go.

I think I hear someone, something, running after me.

Faster! Faster!

One block to go. I can see my house at the end of the road.

Something must be running after me. I can hear him/her/it grunting and laughing.

Faster! Faster!

At least I'm close enough to scream if something takes a bite out of me.

But would Dad come out? Maybe he'd just look out the window and see the monster riding my bike, carrying me back to the monastery.

I get to our driveway and race into the garage. I jump off the bike without stopping and lunge for the kitchen door. I slam the door behind me and lean on it.

Safe.

I catch my breath in huge gulps of air. The kitchen feels good, especially with the light on.

But couldn't a cannibal follow me home and smash his strong hands through the door to pull my head off?

I back away from the door and walk into the middle of the kitchen, closer to the light.

Everything seems too normal inside. Dad is outside on the patio, barbecuing hamburgers.

I can hear Mom and my older sister, Kathy, in the den, watching TV.

Don't they know that another grave has been made on the hill? Another victim has been a meal for the monk cannibals? Kathy couldn't care less. She's in high school and only worries about phone calls and TV.

Dad walks in, holding a tray of his well-done patties.

"How's it going, Mike?"

What a stupid question. Maybe I should tell the truth: Great, Dad. Do you remember the people next-door? Well, they were last night's meal up at the monastery. I understand we might be dessert.

But it wouldn't make much sense to ruin such a nice spring evening with such disastrous news. I mean, what would Miss Manners say of such dinner topics?

"Okay," I answer.

"Fine," he says as he places the burgers on the table. "Will you get Kathy and Mom?"

"Sure."

I look at the plates of charred meat. I wonder what is being served at the monastery's table tonight. Maybe a plate of roast boy's leg and a side order of mashed brains.

Perhaps the cook is telling all the cannibals in the monastery that it's time to eat.

I couldn't eat much tonight, except for the ice cream. For some reason, the juicy burgers didn't look right. I would become a vegetarian, but I don't like vegetables.

Kathy and I were sent to bed an hour ago, but I'm still looking out my window at the monastery. The tower sticks out and looks down at the neighborhood.

Maybe I should tell Dad about the new grave. He could call the police, and the governor would be notified. Eventually a new weapon would be tested on the cannibals to see if they would die.

But what if the new weapon makes the cannibals

stronger and more evil? That means they would need more young boys to eat.

I better not tell Dad.

He'd laugh at me, anyway. He always does. He and Mom think I have too much of an imagination. When I told them that my teacher, Mrs. Harcrow, can ride a broom in the air, my mom laughed so hard that she got tears in her eyes.

They say I should write comedy when I grow up. But what chance does a boy in this neighborhood have of growing up? I might be number fourteen.

But who is number thirteen? Maybe we could go door-to-door in the neighborhood and ask all the parents if they're missing a boy. It seems like a young boy would be missed in a day or two.

I look up at the monastery again. The cannibals are probably turning into bats right now. They'll be squeaking around the neighborhood, trying to decide who'll be number fourteen.

I turn over and look at my night-light, then pull the covers over my head.

"Just three more months," I mumble to myself. "Just three more months."

3
Who's Number Thirteen?

Who is, or was, number thirteen?

Kenny, Pratt, and I spent the entire weekend calling everybody in the neighborhood. But no one was missing.

Glen Brown was gone to visit his grandmother in Florida, but his mom told us she just talked to him Saturday morning.

Glen was crossed off the list.

"What about Ralph?" Kenny says, looking at our list of eight-year-olds.

"Too young," Pratt answers. "We got to concentrate on nine- and ten-year-olds."

Kenny draws a line through the eight-year-olds list.

"Should we call the police?" I ask.

"Nah," says Pratt. "They only concern themselves with important crimes."

"But isn't eating a person a crime?" Kenny wonders.

"Sure, if the person is at least a teenager," Pratt says.

I thought how sad this must be for number thirteen. He was the main course for a bunch of red-eyed, boy-eating monks, and no one is even concerned. It seems like he would deserve more than a one-day search.

We look at our list again. Most of the names are crossed off. We'll have to wait for Monday and check out the remaining names at school.

Monday is a warm day, and on warm days Mrs. Liffreth, our principal, lets us take our sack lunches outside to eat. Summer vacation is only a month away, and the warm weather makes me wish that today was the last day of school.

I meet Kenny out by the back fence of the school yard to eat lunch. We get into a big discussion about how flying saucers can fly without jet engines. Kenny amazes me with how little he knows about space travel. He's never heard of antigravity gasoline.

Pratt walks over, eating one of the apples from his lunch box. His mom is always packing extra fruit and vegetables in his lunch so that he can snack during the day—something about his metabolism. He says he isn't fat, though. He just has big bones.

Big bones must have a lot of fat around them.

Kenny makes fun of Pratt's lunch. He calls it Pratt's hippo food because hippos eat a lot of vegetables and grass.

I don't know why Pratt's mom thinks that all those vegetables and fruits will help him lose weight. I've never seen a skinny hippo.

After he takes the last bite of his apple, Pratt throws it into his sack and wipes off his mouth.

"It's Val," Pratt says, licking off the sticky apple juice from his fingers.

Kenny and I look at each other, confused.

"Val?" Kenny asks.

Pratt rolls his eyes and bangs the back of his head on the fence.

"Don't be so stupid!" Pratt moans. "He's number thirteen."

"You sure?" I ask.

"He wasn't in his class today. Sue said something about he was home sick."

"Or in the garden," I say, almost smiling. I don't care too much for Val, anyway. He is, that is, *was* the smartest kid in the school. He should be in Mrs. Harcrow's class, but everyone thought he was too smart for fourth grade, so they put him with us in Mr. Vernelli's fifth-grade class.

Last year Val won the state elementary math contest. That's all the rest of us heard from our parents for weeks. "Why can't you be like that Mangus kid?"

Val became the least-liked kid in school. One day Ben Galvin, the dumbest kid in school, chased Val all around the playground. It didn't matter, though. Ben is so stupid that he wouldn't have known what to do if he caught Val, anyway. But I'm sure the rest of us could have given him some ideas.

And now Val is number thirteen. I wonder if the cannibals will get smarter after eating him. I heard somewhere that when rats were fed the brains of other, smart rats, they became smart, too.

That's all we need, smart cannibals. They can now keep track of their victims with computer programs. Maybe they'll start going to school and learn how to read: See Val run. See Val cook. Cook, Val, cook. Val smells good. Val tastes good.

One thing this world doesn't need is a smart cannibal.

But all our hopes are ruined when Frank Lewis tells us that he saw Val on Sunday. Apparently, Val was working on a science project in his backyard. Something about a laser weapon.

So Val wasn't number thirteen after all. But who is? That's all we talk about as we ride home on our bikes.

"Did you check any of the fifth graders?" I ask.

"Nah," Pratt answers. "Most fifth graders are older than ten."

"Maybe cannibals can eat eleven-year-olds," Kenny wonders. "Maybe they just have to cook them longer, or something."

"Don't you know anything?" Pratt says. "When you become eleven, your body goes through the change."

Pratt knows all about the facts of life, so we never argue with him. Although I wonder what change would make a fifth grader so distasteful to a cannibal.

After dinner, I watch the evening news. It seems that something would be reported about a lost boy, especially if the police suspected that a monastery full of cannibals ate him for dinner.

But not a word. Only a story about the school budget, some guy suing the city because he was fired, the vice president coming to town, a fire destroying millions of dollars downtown. Unimportant stories like that. Nothing about cannibals.

Why are the police so secretive about the monastery? Why hasn't Tom Brokaw grabbed a news camera and a microphone and gotten the story of the boy-eating monks? Maybe no one cares about chewed-up boys. Except, of course, other boys.

I get a pencil and some paper and write down every boy I know at school. Some boys I know only by looks, so I write "big freckles" or "curly red hair" on the paper. Tomorrow I can go to school and check off each boy on the list as I see him.

It's late when I get my list done. I reach over and turn off the lamp.

I look out my window and see the dark tower sticking up from the gloomy monastery.

It must have been days since number thirteen was eaten. They must be getting hungry enough to look for number fourteen. They'll be going into boys' rooms and poking ribs and feeling legs like they were at a grocery store.

Unless, of course, the boy has a light on in his room—I reach over and turn on my night-light—and is protected by some covers. I crawl under my blanket.

The rest of the week is spent searching for who could be number thirteen. For a while we have it narrowed down to Cliff Jones. No one has seen him for three weeks. But we have to cross off Cliff when we find out that he moved to a different town.

No one is missing.

Maybe the boy was from a different school. In that case, who cares? We let the whole thing drop. It's Friday again, and we have a whole weekend to look forward to. The last thing we needed to concern ourselves with is a missing boy from a different school.

4
"It's Your Turn"

As usual on Friday, Kenny, Pratt, and I take the long way home on our bikes. It's the only day our parents don't expect us to come straight home from school.

When we finally get to our neighborhood, we see Jenny walking with Kimberly.

"Hey, lardhead," Pratt yells to Jenny. He likes her a lot.

Jenny turns around and frowns at Pratt. "Drop dead, Horton!" She likes Pratt.

Kenny rides up onto the sidewalk and stops quickly in front of the girls.

"Hey, look what escaped from the zoo," Kenny says. Kenny likes Jenny the best.

Jenny and Kimberly walk around Kenny.

"Don't you have to have a license to look that ugly?" Jenny yells back to Kenny. She likes Kenny the best, too.

Pratt passes Kenny and rides up behind Kimberly and Jenny. Jenny is acting perturbed, but she's probably loving the attention. She stops and swings around.

"You think you're good on that bike?" she asks.

"The best in the neighborhood." Pratt smiles.

She looks over to Kenny and me.

"I bet Mike and Kenny could beat you."

I feel flattered, but a little bit ashamed. I know better.

Pratt looks over at us and smiles. "Those two? They couldn't beat me if I had two flat tires."

That makes me mad. It may be true, but it still makes me mad.

"I've beaten you before," I protest.

"Not since I had my broken foot."

And that was quite a while ago. And even with his foot in a cast, I didn't beat him by much.

Pratt rides onto the road and swings around.

"Watch this," he says to Jenny.

Kimberly isn't impressed as Pratt spins on one wheel. Why should she be?—snobs are never impressed.

Pratt stops his spinning and realizes that neither of the girls cares about his fancy tricks. He's got to find something else to get Jenny to notice him.

"Get over here, guys," he says to Kenny and me.

Kenny and I would rather not race, at least not today. It's bad enough to lose all the time, but it's even worse when you lose in front of Jenny.

But it would be worst of all to chicken out and not race at all. We ride up next to Pratt. We'd rather die trying than chicken out.

In fact, dying would make a great impression on Jenny. Well, not dying, but crashing good enough to get her attention. I could hit the curb and go flying into the streetlight. If I hit it hard enough, blood would drip from a large gash on my forehead. Jenny would run up to me and hold me. She'd tell me how sorry she was that I got hurt. She wouldn't even notice that Pratt was at the top of Ash Street and had won the race.

I'm sure Kenny is thinking the same thing. He's probably planning to hit the curb also. But what if we both hit the curb? Would she go to Kenny or me? It would be bad enough to be wounded and bleeding. But it would be worse if she ran to Kenny first. That would be embarrassing. Maybe crashing isn't the best idea.

"First one to the top wins," yells Pratt. "Last one walks the wall." He turns to Jenny. "Watch this."

He turns back and looks up the road. We all hug close to our bikes, one foot on the ground and one on the pedal. We look like coiled springs ready to unwind.

"Start us, Kenny," Pratt says.

"On your mark, get set, go!"

I push off. In less than a second, all of us are standing on our pedals and hunched over the handlebars.

This race is for all the glory. It's for Jenny.

I've seen shows on TV where moose fight each other for their girlfriends. Perhaps it would be better if they had bikes so that they could just race to see who wins. But I don't think moose could learn how to ride bikes.

For the first block we're all close together. But my legs are already tired.

As we turn up Ash Street, I glance down the road to

see how Jenny and Kimberly are enjoying our race.

They aren't even watching! They're walking into Jenny's house. Maybe we should call the race off. Why hurt our legs and lungs while the girls we're trying to impress have gone inside a house to eat an after-school snack?

Do girl moose go off and eat grass while the boy moose risk their lives for them? Maybe all this stuff about impressing girls would stop if boys noticed that the girls couldn't care less.

But it's too late. We're at the bottom of Ash Street and on our way up. No one's going to call it off now. Not even for two girls who are eating a snack. As usual, Pratt is in front and I'm fighting to stay in second place. Kenny is trailing behind.

As we get near the top of Ash Street, the tower of the monastery sticks up higher. I pedal a little harder. I don't want to walk the wall tonight.

Suddenly Kenny whizzes by me! He's pedaling faster than I've ever seen him before. His teeth are clenched together. He knows he's pedaling for his life.

The last two times on the wall were not good for him. Maybe the third time would be disastrous. And it would be awful to be number fourteen without knowing who number thirteen was.

He even passes Pratt! Pratt is so shocked that he almost stops in the middle of the road.

All of a sudden I'm in third place.

The wall!

Faster! Faster!

It's no use. Kenny's already at the top, looking down, and Pratt is just about there.

I slow down. No use hurting my legs anymore. I'll need all my strength to walk the wall. I pedal slowly to the top, where Kenny and Pratt wait.

Kenny is smiling as he huffs and puffs, trying to catch his breath. He looks relieved that he won't have to try the wall for a third time.

"Whoo-eee," Pratt yells. "Did you see Kenny turn on the juice?"

Kenny looks down at me. "It's your turn today."

It's my turn, all on account of some stupid girls. I'll be walking the wall, the wall between life and death, while the girls munch on crackers and peanut butter.

I bet moose don't feel this stupid.

Pratt turns onto Sunset Drive and heads for the monastery. "Who knows, after today there may be fourteen in the garden."

I feel sick.

Kenny gives me a worried look. "You gonna make it?"

I nod my head. My thrill side makes me nod my head. It wants to climb the wall and get close to death. It wants to be number fourteen.

Kenny rides up Sunset Drive and also heads toward the monastery. I take a couple of deep breaths and follow behind. Way behind.

Stupid girls.

5
Attack of the Killer Roses

Pratt and Kenny wait for me at the wall. This is how it must feel to be a car racer, knowing everyone in the stands is hoping you'll crash into a flaming fireball of twisted metal.

I get off my bike and look up at the wall. It's so familiar to me, and yet it looks strange and cold. I've climbed it before, quite a few times. But it still has an eeriness to it.

"Get climbing," Kenny says, still excited with his first-place win.

"Give me a minute."

"Got your will made out?" Pratt laughs.

"Real funny."

I put my hands on the stones. They're cold, like I'd expect a body to feel if it'd been dead for a week. My fingers curl around one of the stones, and I pull myself up. As a precaution, I look over my shoulder to see if I have enough sunlight. The last thing I need right now is for the sun to set while I'm at the top of the wall. I shudder at the thought of standing on the wall with no protective sunlight.

My thrill side can't wait to get on top of the wall. It wants to walk it one more time and take a good look at that new grave.

My feet find small stone ledges to stand on as my hands find more stones to grab above me. I move a few inches at a time. There's no need to hurry. Why would anyone want to hurry to a dinner for which they are going to be the main course?

"Too slow!" Kenny yells up.

"Yeah, well, I think these rocks have moved," I yell back. "I can't climb them as easy."

Kenny walks up to the wall and inspects the stones.

"Nah," he says. "Your feet just grew since the last time you climbed the wall."

I get higher and reach up to grab the top. With one last pull I lift myself onto the top of the wall. I look over to the monastery and down into the garden. I have to be sure that the cannibal monks are safely waiting in their dark corners.

It's safe. No one is outside, but I know I'm being watched from the dark tower. There must be red glaring eyes piercing through the darkness to watch me walk the wall, hoping I'll slip and fall into the boy-eating garden.

They hope for number fourteen.

My thrill side wants to look in the windows and see if a dark shadow floats by again. But I look only at the wall.

I slowly stand up, holding my arms out for balance. So far, so good. At least no one has tried to kill me yet.

I look down at my feet. Once I start walking, I don't want to look down at the garden, where I could break my leg. I have to concentrate on the feet, my only hope for survival.

I start walking, placing each foot only an inch in front of the other.

"Are you sure you're going slow enough?" Pratt says sarcastically.

I ignore him as I inch my feet forward. My arms are stretched out, making me look like a bird trying to land. Out of the corner of my eye I can see Pratt and Kenny walking along the wall beneath me.

My thrill side loves to have an audience.

Slower. Slower.

I can't speed up. My thrill side wants to try to run across the wall. But this time I keep my thrill side under control.

Step by step.

It seems like I've been on the wall for hours, but I've only walked a few feet.

As I try to move my right foot, it stops.

"Oh, no," Kenny gasps.

I look down and see Kenny covering his mouth with his hand, like he was holding back a scream. Pratt looks pale.

I try again to move my right foot, but it's held back. My heart pounds harder and faster.

Something is holding my leg!

I let out a small moan, too scared to look behind me. I tug my leg again, but the thing that is holding me grabs tighter. My only chance is to dive down to Pratt and Kenny.

I swing around and look down at my leg. A killer rose hungrily hangs on, twisting around my pants, sinking its teeth in deeper.

I panic and try to brush the rose off, but it bites my hand.

There's no time to lose! Jump for my life!

As I turn to jump off, my other foot slips, and I fall on my stomach on the wall. Umph!

I can't breathe.

The rose pulls harder, and I slowly slip down into its hungry grip. I see Kenny and Pratt watch in horror as I drift slowly down the wall and into the garden.

With one last pull the roses drag me down to the other side of the wall. I feel weak and lost. With a thud I fall on my back in the middle of the roses.

I hear Kenny scream and Pratt yell. Then I hear them jump onto their bikes and race away from the massacre. Some friends.

I feel the teeth of the roses take bites out of my body. I'm too scared to scream for help. I'm alone in the roses, in the garden of the cannibals.

I lie on the ground and try to catch my breath. It seems so peaceful in the garden. So quiet.

Deathly quiet.

The roses sway above me, triumphantly swinging back and forth. "We've got number fourteen!" they must be yelling to the cannibals inside. Somewhere in the monastery there's a pot with boiling water waiting for me to fill it. A cannibal is probably slicing carrots and onions into the pot.

I hate onions.

Somewhere in the monastery there's dancing and celebrating.

But the garden is quiet.

"Are you okay?"

Who said that? It wasn't Kenny or Pratt. Perhaps a policeman saw me fall into the garden and jumped over the wall to save me from being the main ingredient in boy lasagna.

But it's not a policeman.

Someone else is in the garden!

I lift my head. For the first time I notice an old, withered man wearing a long black robe. He's kneeling over the new grave. Why didn't I see him before? How could I have missed such an obvious danger?

I'm so scared, I can't talk. I'm not even sure I remember how to breathe.

But I'm also mad. Darn you, Pratt! They *can* go out in the sunlight. Their skin doesn't boil. If I get out of here alive, I'm going to punch Pratt in the stomach.

But getting out alive is looking doubtful.

The old man stands up. The robe goes all the way down to the ground. He's holding a pair of garden clippers just like the ones my mom has—the ones they sell on TV for only $9.95.

What the TV ads don't explain is that the trimmers are good for trimming grass, clipping bushes, and butchering little boys who fall into the garden by mistake.

The monk walks toward me. He's old and ugly. His skin is whiter than Mom's Thanksgiving china. He walks over to me with small, painful steps.

I guess he must be over four hundred years old, which would be fairly old even for a cannibal. At least that's what Pratt told me.

But Pratt also told me that cannibals couldn't be out in the sunlight. And yet, here's one walking right toward me now, even with the sun up.

Darn you, Pratt!

The monk-cannibal gets closer. I don't know if I'm breathing or not. I don't know if I hurt or not. All I know is that the monk is walking toward me, a cannibal-monk with a garden weapon in his hand and a taste for young boys.

I feel numb.

When he gets a foot or two away from me, he stops. He looks me over from head to foot. I feel like a piece of fruit in the store that is picked up by all the shoppers to be poked and sniffed to see if it's ripe.

I hope the monk doesn't sniff or thump me. I don't want to die like a cantaloupe.

"Are you all right, son?"

The monster monk speaks again! Not only does it talk, but it talks English. How strange. It doesn't seem right to be eaten by someone who speaks like you do. It seems uncivilized. I mean, would we eat a cow or a pig if we could talk to it? Would we eat a piece of corn if it told us that it didn't want to die in boiling water? I doubt it.

But here the monk talks to me like he was my grandfather.

"I—ah—I guess so," I gasp, realizing that I haven't breathed since I saw him kneeling by the grave.

He gets down on one knee and puts his hands on my leg. His touch gives me the chills. Here he goes, poking me to see if I'm ripe.

"Your leg got pretty scratched up."

I look down at my leg and see where the killer roses took small bites out of me. The thorns have gone through my jeans and are still chewing on my leg. Small red spots of blood dot my pants.

The monk raises his garden weapon and moves toward my leg. I close my eyes, afraid to watch my body be cut up for stew meat. I can feel him tugging on my leg. He must be looking for the best place to make the first cut.

His garden shears snip twice. Each time I cringe and feel weak.

"That should do it," the monk says as he gently takes hold of my leg and lifts it from the cut rose stems.

My eyes are wide with fear as he carefully pulls the last rose stem from my pants. His touch is gentle and caring. But then, anyone picking fruit to eat is careful not to bruise the fruit.

"I knew that would happen one day," he says as he slowly stands up. "I knew that if I didn't cut those roses, one of you boys would get caught."

He looks down at me. There's something in the way his eyes look that makes me feel comfortable. Maybe he's trying to hypnotize me so that I'll walk into the pot of boiling water by myself and soak with the carrots and onions.

I look away.

He reaches out and touches my forehead. I pull back and look at his hand. He has blood on his fingers. I reach up and feel where he touched me. It's wet, sticky, and warm. I pull my hand down and look at the blood covering my fingers, too.

The monk reaches into his robe and pulls out a white cloth. He folds it in half and places it on the cut on my forehead. He takes my hand and places it on the cloth so that I can hold it in place.

"You better keep some pressure on that cut for a while," he says. "I don't think you'll need stitches, but you better come in and lie down."

He stands up and takes my other arm and helps me stand. He pulls me toward a door leading into the monastery. He's leading me into the cannibal restaurant!

I tug my arm out of his grip and stop. He looks back at me and gives me a confused look. "Are you sure you are all right?"

"Fine—ah—fine," I say, searching for some excuse. "I better get home. My mom and dad are expecting me."

"I could call them and have them pick you up."

Pick me up? Who's this cannibal trying to fool? That way he could have the entire Cummings family for dinner. Mom for the appetizer, me for the main course, Dad for dessert, and Kathy for a before-bed snack.

"No, no. That's okay. I can get home all right."

"Are you sure?" he says, looking at me with those old, comfortable eyes.

I look away. "Sure. I'm fine." I walk over to the wall and start climbing the stones.

"Wait," the monk yells over to me. "You can go through the front gate. You don't have to climb the wall."

Another ploy to get me to go through the monastery, where his clan of cannibals waits in the kitchen for the main part of the menu—me!

"My bike's right over here."

I climb up without looking back. I can't look at his eyes anymore. They may convince me that I should stay and lie down in the monastery. Wait for the water to come to a full boil before I'm placed in it.

They may convince me to be number fourteen.

I make it to the top and jump down to the other side.

Free! I did it! I fell into the garden and lived to tell about it. They should make a T-shirt that says, I Fell off the Wall and Survived.

Pratt and Kenny are nowhere around. They left me for dead as soon as I fell. Some friends.

I get on my bike and pedal away as fast as I can. The breeze feels good on my cut forehead. Then I remember the cloth I'm holding in my hand. I hold it up and look at it. It's not a rag from some old pillowcase. It's beautiful, with gold edging.

A gift from a cannibal.

★ ★ ★

I lean on my elbows on my bed and look up at the monastery on the hill. I should have gone to sleep an hour ago, but the monastery keeps me awake.

The lump on my head is throbbing. Mom and Dad bought my story of falling off my bike. I thought it would be better to lie than to explain my narrow escape from hungry cannibals.

I keep my night-light on, even though I'm not sure if the light bothers cannibals. If the sun doesn't melt their flesh, I doubt my four-watt light bulb is going to hurt them.

No sense wasting electricity, so I click the light off.

I look down as I fold, open, then refold the beautiful handkerchief. The moonlight drifting through the window makes the gold edges glitter. My fingers run along the edge until they get to one corner, where the initials T. L. are sewn in.

T. L.? What could that stand for? Does the cannibal have a name? Maybe Tom Lewis.

Nah. Tom isn't the type of name for someone who eats young boys. It must be something weird, like Treebow Lipzerek—something from another country. Or planet.

6
The Curse of the Handkerchief

The old cannibal walks up to me, hungry for young boy flesh. He smiles with a sick, devilish grin as he limps closer. He snaps his grass trimmers above his head.

The roses hold me tight, like a bug in a spider's web. The harder I try to escape, the tighter the roses twist around me.

The cannibal reaches out and grabs my arm. He shakes it, trying to break it off my body so that he can eat me piece by piece!

I try to scream, but I can't.

He shakes harder. . . .

"Mike, get up."

Someone is shaking my arm.

"It's Pratt; he's on the phone."

I open my eyes and look up to see Mom shaking my arm.

What a relief. Moms are always better to look at than cannibals.

"Who?" I ask, still groggy with sleep.

"Pratt. I told him you were still asleep, but he wanted me to check anyway. He sounds frantic; you better go talk to him."

As I sit up, all the blood pounds into the lump on my forehead. It hurts so bad that I have to lie down again. After a moment of moaning, I sit up very slowly. I let the lump fill up only a bit at a time. That way it doesn't feel like it's going to burst.

I swing my feet out from under the warm blankets and plop them onto the floor. My legs feel sore from all the rose bites. I sit on the edge of the bed for a few seconds to get enough blood in my brain to make walking possible.

"Hurry; he really sounds worried," Mom says as she walks out of the room.

I stand up and walk out into the hallway, but my knees want to buckle under me.

I get to the kitchen and pick up the phone from the counter.

"Hello."

There's a pause. I can hear Pratt breathing.

"This really you, Mike?" he says with a shaky voice.

I sit on the carpet to rest my sore legs. "Course it is."

I hear him sigh with relief. "Oh, man, I thought that was it for you. I thought you were going to be—"

"Number fourteen?"

"Yeah, well you know, when you fell in . . ."

"And where did you go?" I ask, trying to sound mad.

"We went to get help," Pratt says defensively.

"Help? You never got any help."

Pratt is silent for a while. I can tell he's embarrassed. He knows that he rode home as fast as he could and locked himself into his bedroom, turned on his light, and climbed under his blanket.

But little did he know that the light probably wasn't going to help him at all. I'm not sure about the blanket, but I know that the light wouldn't keep any cannibals away.

"How'd you get out?" he asks curiously.

"I climbed out."

"Did you see anything?"

"One of the monks. He was kneeling by the new grave when I fell in."

"And you got out?" Pratt yells with amazement.

"Sure. He came over and helped me get out of the roses."

"He helped you?"

Pratt's voice is getting higher and louder with each question. I think it won't be long until his voice cracks.

"Yeah. He even gave me a handkerchief to put on my head."

Pratt is silent for a moment. "He gave you what?" he asks in a low and concerned voice.

"A handkerchief."

"I'll be right over."

He hangs up the phone. The phone goes dead, and the buzz makes the lump on my forehead ache. I reach up and touch the sore and gently rub the golf-ball–sized lump just under my hairline. It throbs when I touch it, and I flinch with pain. It probably looks like one of those bumps that Elmer Fudd gets when Bugs Bunny hits him on the head.

I stand up to hang up the phone and walk into the bathroom. Looking in the mirror, I pull my hair back to reveal a large, purple lump with a cut in the middle of it. I look like a cookie with a large chocolate chip in the middle.

I go back to my room and search for the handkerchief. It has to be somewhere in my bed. I find it near the bottom, all wadded up in a red, gold, and white ball. I pull it out flat and look at the gold trim. My fingers trace across the pretty T. L. in the corner.

It's a beautiful handkerchief, but also worn out. The red blood spot in the middle of the cloth seems to give the handkerchief a strange beauty.

"Let's see it," Pratt demands even before his bike comes to a stop in my driveway. Kenny is right next to him, looking at me like I've come back from the dead.

I pull out the handkerchief and hand it to Pratt. He just rolls backward on his bike like the cloth was a skunk.

"Get it away from me!" Pratt yells.

What could be so scary about the cloth? What would make Pratt and Kenny back away from such a simple piece of fabric? Maybe the bright-red blood spot.

"It's only a bit of my blood," I reassure them, lifting the handkerchief up higher.

They back up further.

"You nuts?" Pratt screams. "I just wanted to see it, not touch it!"

"It's just a handkerchief," I say as I dangle the horrifying piece of cloth in Pratt's face. I enjoy having such power over him.

Kenny runs backward, staring at the monk's handkerchief.

"Just a cloth, my fanny!" Kenny says. "Whoever has that can be found!"

"You're crazy," I say, but a cold tingle goes down my spine. "He could of got me right there in the garden. Why would he need to track me down later?"

Pratt thinks for a moment, then his eyes light up. "He's hoping you lead him to more young boys to eat. Maybe he eats a bunch at a time."

Maybe the cannibal has a cold meat locker like they have down at the grocery store. But instead of sides of beef hanging on hooks, young boys would be dangling upside down.

I hold the handkerchief away from me. One thing I wouldn't like is to be hanging upside down in a cold locker.

"What do I do with it?" I ask frantically.

"Burn it," Kenny yells from a safe distance.

"No," says Pratt. "It needs to be taken back to the monastery."

Kenny is already shaking his head. "You're nuts. If

we go back there, we're sure to be the next three graves."

Pratt jumps back onto his bike and looks at me as if I'm causing a lot of trouble. "It's got to be done, and it's got to be done soon."

7
Removing the Curse

Man, no way am I going to go in there," Kenny says as we look through the tall iron gate at the front of the monastery. This is the only way in—or out—of the monastery. Unless, of course, you fall into the garden from the wall.

We look through the gate. The stone path leading to the monastery's wooden door cuts through the middle of the front courtyard. The grass in the courtyard is long and needs a cut. A few large oak trees in the court-yard and bushes along the wall block as much of the sun as possible.

I pull the wadded handkerchief out of my pocket. "Let's just throw it over and get out of here." I begin my windup, but Pratt grabs my arm before I can throw.

"No. We got to bury it right next to the monastery."

"Why can't he just throw it over?" Kenny says, look-ing up at the tower.

"Don't you know nothing?" Pratt says. "Anything bad has to be buried."

"Well," Kenny says, "Mike should have to do it. He's the one who fell into the garden and started all this."

"I'm not going in alone," I state firmly. "I'll put it in one of your mailboxes before I go in there alone."

"That's blackmail!" Kenny yells.

"Sh!" Pratt tries to quiet us. "There's nothing to worry about. It's too early in the morning for them to be even awake."

Pratt's right. It's only ten o'clock. The monks would still be snoring away in their coffins up in the tower.

"Let's get this over with," I say as I slowly push the gate open. I'm sort of surprised the gate isn't locked. But why would cannibal monks lock their doors? No one is going to come in.

Except, of course, three real stupid boys.

The gate squeaks so loud that Kenny and Pratt fall into line behind me.

"You want every monk to wake up?" Kenny whispers angrily from behind Pratt.

I stop pushing for a while. The gate probably hasn't been opened for more than a hundred years. I push the gate again, stopping after each inch. The squeaks get louder with each push. Pratt looks up at the tower to make sure no eyes are looking down at us.

I push the gate one last time. It's open enough for us to barely squeeze through. I don't want to push my luck and open it any more.

"Go ahead," I say to Pratt as I step aside and point the way through the gate.

Pratt grabs my arm and pulls me back. "You're the one with the cloth. You first."

I look over to Kenny. The way he's shivering, there's

no way I can convince him to go first. I take a deep breath, suck in my stomach, and squeeze through the small crack in the gate. Pratt and Kenny hold their breaths until I get all the way through without squeaking the gate any more.

Once inside the courtyard, I run behind one of the big oaks. I look through the gate and motion Pratt and Kenny to come in. For a moment it appears that they might jump onto their bikes and leave me again.

"Come on, you chickens," I whisper. Pratt takes a worried look up at the tower. He takes a big breath and squeezes through the gate. He's a bit bigger than me and can't get completely through without moving the gate with a loud squeak. He freezes and starts to sweat. Kenny ducks behind the wall, and I plug my ears with my fingers.

After he's sure nothing has swooped out of the bell tower, Pratt squeezes the rest of the way through. He looks pale and weak as he walks over to me.

Kenny peeks around the wall, knowing that it's his turn to enter the dreaded courtyard. We know he's thinking of some excuse. Pratt scowls at him and waves for him to come in.

Kenny closes his eyes for a moment, then squeezes himself through the gate. He's smaller than Pratt, so he makes it without a peep, much to the relief of Pratt and me.

With all three of us in the courtyard, we look at one another. We look lost and confused. Here we are, but what do we do now? We huddle close together, almost nose to nose.

"Where do we bury it?" Kenny asks in his smallest whisper.

Pratt looks around the oak and points over to the side of the monastery. There's a narrow strip of grass that leads to the garden in back.

"There."

Kenny and I look over to where he points. It's right next to the tower.

Pratt crouches down and walks over to the side of the monastery. I grab Kenny's arm and follow. With Kenny by my side, I figure I have at least a fifty-fifty chance of anything swooping out of the tower grabbing Kenny first. He's probably thinking the same thing.

Pratt sits with his back against the wall. Right above him is a large window. Kenny and I fall down onto our bellies and crawl the rest of the way to Pratt.

We all lean against the wall, panting and sweating. Pratt nervously looks around while I look up at the tower to make sure everyone is still asleep.

"This is stupid," Kenny says in a not-quiet-enough whisper.

"Sh," Pratt and I hiss together.

"Find a stick," Pratt says. "We need to dig a hole here."

The three of us start scurrying around the ground, looking for a big enough stick to dig the hole. But my thrill side is more interested in the window. It's come this far, and it has just got to see what's inside this building.

I slowly lift myself up and look in. Pratt and Kenny

also stand up and put their heads up by the glass.

Through the window we see a large hallway with a bunch of closed doors on the other side. It's dark inside. The sun coming in from the window is the only light in the monastery.

"I wonder where all those doors go to?" I ask.

"Probably to where they eat all the boys," says Pratt.

"I bet they're closets full of heads," Kenny says.

On the wall is a carving of Jesus on the cross. Not exactly the sort of thing you'd expect to see where boys are being eaten and heads being removed and placed in closets.

"I thought cannibals couldn't be near a cross," I say to Pratt.

Pratt takes a minute on this one. He knows as well as anybody that vampires get real sick if they see a cross. And everybody knows that cannibal monks are close relatives of vampires.

"Hello, boys."

A voice!

I look at Pratt; Pratt looks at me. Both of us look at Kenny, who's too scared to look at anyone.

It was a voice, but not one of ours. Worse yet, it was behind us.

Now is the time to act, not think. The last thing any of us wants to do is turn around and see who, or what, said hello.

Pratt runs for the gate without even looking back.

The only thing between Kenny and the front gate is me, so Kenny shoves me to the ground and runs over me, screaming all the way out the gate.

I can hear them escape on their bikes. Again.

I jump up, but before I take a step, something grabs my shoulder. My body turns to ice. I can't move. I only stare at the front gate. On my shoulder I can feel a hand. It's heavy. I turn my head slowly and see a gnarled, old hand resting on my shoulder. Its skin almost looks like white glass with brown spots in it. It's old, at least a couple of hundred years, and it has me.

The hand turns me around until I'm face to face with the same old man I saw in the garden yesterday. He is so stooped with age, which I guess to be 453, that his body looks like it's having a losing fight with gravity. He's wearing the same black robe I saw him with yesterday. Obviously, this old man hasn't been out shopping for a while.

He recognizes me and smiles, showing a set of very yellow teeth. Teeth which have probably taken more than one bite out of a young boy.

"You're the boy who fell into the garden yesterday," he says.

My brain is screaming at me. It wants me to yell, holler, say something. My dad says I can always talk my way out of anything. But now I can't speak. I only nod my head.

"Your friends don't seem to stay around long," he says, looking over to the front gate.

Finally I can feel my brain feeding some words to my mouth.

"They went to get the national guard," I finally blurt out.

The monk looks surprised. His grin gets wider and the teeth get yellower. I don't think he believes my story.

He looks down at my hand and sees his handkerchief. I look down and unfold the bloodstained cloth.

"I just wanted to return this," I say as I hand him the cloth.

He takes it carefully and runs his old, swollen fingers along the gold edge. He looks at the red spot in the middle then looks up at my forehead. He's not smiling anymore. He looks concerned.

He reaches up and tries to move my hair from the lump on my forehead. I pull back, but his hand on my shoulder doesn't let me go far. He gently touches my bump. I expected to scream with pain, but his fingers are gentle.

"Are you better?" he asks.

I just nod my head, too afraid to say much more. All I have to tell him is my name, age, and phone number. I think about Pratt and Kenny and how I'm going to kill them when (if) I ever get out of here.

The old man grabs ahold of my arm. "Come inside for a moment. I have something for you."

He starts walking toward the front of the monastery, using me as some sort of human crutch. I can hear fossilized bones crackle as he walks. He's breathing hard, as if walking is something he isn't used to.

I'm sure flying is much easier for him, as it would be for all bat-flying, boy-eating cannibals.

He walks me over to the stone path leading up to the wooden front door. As we start walking toward the door, I try to imagine what this ancient thing has to show me. Most likely a large pot of boiling water. I must be the last needed ingredient for boy spaghetti.

We get to the first step of the path. He stops and lifts his foot. In one careless moment, his death grip loosens. Now's my chance! I look behind me to the open gate. In one smooth move, I yank my arm from his grip and turn toward the gate.

"Wait!" the monk yells.

As I run out through the gate, I glance back at my would-be captor. He tries to balance his withered body on the step, his face showing the pain of all his bones crunching together.

Safely outside, I grab my bike and run with it down Sunset Drive. Within seconds I'm flying along on my bike toward the park. I know Kenny and Pratt would hide under the bridge by the creek. They're probably deciding what they should tell my mom and dad.

I get to the park and ride over the bridge. On the other side is a steep path leading down to the small creek under the bridge. Usually it's better to take the path slowly. But since I'm racing away from cannibals, I ride down the path as fast as I can.

A bump throws me off the bike, and I tumble off to

the side. The bike continues down the path and splashes into the water. I roll over to see Kenny and Pratt crouching under the bridge, their eyes wide with fear.

"Mike?" Kenny asks.

I try to lift up, but the bumps and bruises in and on my body pull me back down to the ground. I groan.

They slowly come out from under the bridge and walk toward me. But they don't get too close.

Pratt leans forward, but not too far forward. "You all right?"

"Yeah, I think so," I say as I try to sit up.

Kenny and Pratt back up a bit.

This has been a rotten couple of days. If things keep going like they have been, there won't be much left of me for the cannibals to eat.

"That's it. I've had enough," I say as I stand up and pick out the leaves and twigs from my hair. "I'm not going back to that monastery for the rest of my life."

"Where's the handkerchief?" Kenny asks.

"The old monk has it. I gave it back."

I pull my bike out of the stream and pull a small branch from the spokes. Pratt runs up beside me.

"But you've got to burn it!"

"You don't know what you're talking about," I yell back angrily. "You haven't been right about anything. First you tell me to bury it; now you say burn it!"

I can tell Pratt is hurt. His face is a bright red and the freckles on his face look dark orange.

"Yeah, well . . . I got you out of there alive," he says.

"You?" I yell. "You guys ran away both times and left me alone with that old man."

Kenny is ashamed and looks down at his feet while Pratt tries to think of something to say.

"I'm through with that place," I say as I push my bike up the hill.

8
He Finds Me

Sunday afternoons are always quiet. And with the smell of hot bread in the house, this Sunday is even more enjoyable. Mom says she doesn't like making bread, but since her mom used to bake it, she feels like she has to also.

Mom is always doing something because she feels guilty. And that's fine with me. I love her wheat-nut bread.

"There's a real old man walking up the driveway," Kathy says.

Dad puts down his paper to look out the window.

"And he's wearing an old blanket," she adds.

My stomach falls and I start to breathe funny. An old man wearing a blanket? Could he have found me? Would he try to do something to me with my family watching? Even on Sunday?

How did he know where I live? He must have looked down from his evil tower and watched as I pedaled home. In most cases the cannibals would wait for dinner to come to them. But if they were hungry enough, they would probably go out and find someone ripe enough to eat.

I roll off the couch and race upstairs into the bathroom. I slam the door behind me and lock it. I lean on the door and collapse onto the floor. He's found me.

The doorbell rings.

"No," I whisper to myself. Kathy is probably going to the door now. "No, don't do it."

I hear the door open. That stupid girl has opened the door! She's leaving the door open so that the cannibal can fly in and find me. I've escaped him twice, but now he's decided not to let me get away a third time.

I wait for the screams, but all I can hear are some muffled voices. It even sounds like my dad and the monk are having a pleasant conversation.

"Hello, Mr. Cummings. I've come to eat your son."

"How nice. Won't you come in. I'll go get him."

Maybe those aren't the exact words, but that's what it sounds like to me.

"Mike?" Dad calls up to me. "Someone is here for you."

I feel like throwing up. My own dad wants me to go with the boy-eating monk. Dad always said that life would be easier in the house without me, but I never thought he would let me die in such a tasty manner.

"Mike?"

Footsteps! Someone is walking up the stairs. They're coming to get me. I'm sure Kathy is even telling them where I am. She always said I was a pest. Obviously, if I was cooked up in some cannibal pie, I wouldn't be much of a pest anymore.

Someone knocks on the bathroom door, and my spine shivers out through my skin. I stop breathing.

"Mike?" my dad calls. "You in there?"

"Yeah," I say, my voice squeaking.

"There's someone here to see you."

"I don't feel real good."

"But he's got something for you."

"I'm real sick."

"What's wrong?"

"Nothing. I'm just too sick to come out now."

I can hear Dad standing out by the door for a moment. He's trying to think of what to tell the old man downstairs. I'm sorry, but he's too sick to be eaten today, perhaps tomorrow—or something like that.

He walks back downstairs. I press my ear to the door. All I can hear is "Smells good," "Thank you," and "Have a nice day."

The front door shuts. I wait by the bathroom door for a while to make sure that the old man has left. I start to breathe again.

I unlock the door and open it slowly. I stick my head out first. Everything smells and sounds like a normal Sunday afternoon again.

I stand up and carefully walk downstairs.

Dad is sitting on the couch with the sports section of the paper. Kathy is reading the comics. The old man is nowhere to be seen. I walk the rest of the way down and into the living room.

"You feeling better?" Dad asks, putting down the paper.

"Yeah—uh—a little," I say as I sit back down on the couch.

"That was Father Lawrence."

"Who?"

"Father Lawrence. The monk who lives up in the monastery."

"He has a name?" I ask, surprised that a cannibal would have such a normal name.

Dad starts laughing. "Sure. What did you expect?"

What a weird name for a cannibal. The greatest fear of my young life has a goofy name. I feel a little stupid being afraid of a person named Lawrence.

I expected Doctor Death or Mr. Ripper.

Not Father Lawrence.

"He's a dad?" I ask.

"No, a Father," Dad says. "All monks are called either Father or Brother."

Dad holds out his hand. In his palm is my lucky coin. "He said you lost this in his garden. He thought it might be something special."

I pick the coin up out of Dad's hand and feel the edges. "He came by just to give me this?"

"I guess so," Dad says. He goes back to reading his paper.

It doesn't make sense. The old man walking all the way down to my house just to return my lucky coin.

I rub my fingers on the face of Ben Franklin, wondering why the old monk would take time to find a boy who fell into his garden just to return a stupid lucky coin. For some reason, the old monk has taken a special interest in me. Perhaps he wants to get to know my family better before he takes me away for food.

Maybe Dad and Mom will become friends with him. All he would have to do is ask.

"Since Mike is such a bother at home, why don't you let me have him?" the monk would ask over coffee and cake.

Mom and Dad would look at each other and smile. "Yes, he would be better off as a casserole than a teenager."

Or perhaps Dad would lose me in a friendly game of poker with the monk. Dad should know better than to play cards with cannibals. They cheat.

I decide I need to become the best-behaved son in the world. From now on, I'll do just what Mom and Dad tell me to do. And I'll do it before they remind me for the fourth time. That way Mom and Dad just might want to keep me.

Mom walks into the living room with a loaf of her bread.

"Take this up to the monastery," she says, handing me the warm loaf.

"The monastery?" I ask, starting to get sick again.

"Sure. Father Lawrence sounded like he would like nothing better than a piece of homemade bread."

Mom's way off base here. What the old monk would like is a nice piece of boy meat between two slices of warm, homemade bread. And Mom even wants me to deliver both to the monk.

"I don't feel very good," I honestly say.

Dad puts down his paper and looks at me. "I thought you said you were feeling better."

"Yeah. Better, but not good enough to walk up the hill to the monastery."

I bend over and fake a few groans. There is no way I'm going to deliver a full meal to that ancient cannibal.

Mom gives the loaf to Kathy. "Here, you take it."

Kathy looks up from the comics and gives Mom a dirty look. "Why me?"

"Mike doesn't feel well enough," Mom says, going back to the kitchen.

"But that place is creepy," she protests.

Kathy looks down at the loaf, then up at me. I can tell by her scowl that she isn't real happy with me. "You just want to be sick so you don't have to do anything."

She jumps up and stomps out the front door with the loaf under her arm. The door slams behind her.

The idea of Kathy walking into the lair of cannibal fiends makes me smile. I think of all the times she's called me a brat, or a toad-eating geek. And now she's walking toward the monastery with a loaf of freshly made bread. The smell of that bread is going to make the monks forget all about Kathy being a girl. They're going to grab the loaf and Kathy and throw them both onto the bread counter to be sliced for sandwiches.

It makes me smirk.

I excuse myself and walk upstairs. My room is at the end of the hall, and I have to pass Kathy's room to get to mine. As I pass her room, I look inside. Kathy has, or had, a nice stereo and lots of CDs. She never lets me listen to them. But now that she's going to become a Sunday snack for some hungry monks, no sense letting Mom and Dad throw her stuff away.

I walk in and scout around. "CD player, CDs," I say to myself as I make a mental note of what I'll take when she's gone.

"Books." I look down at her shelf of paperbacks. Most of the books seem too dumb or too hard. I'll let the Salvation Army come get the books.

But the CDs and the CD player are mine. I'll be tactful. I'll wait until Mom and Dad's grief for Kathy is over before I ask for her things. That should be at least until the day after tomorrow.

On her nightstand is a group of pictures. Mostly of herself. That figures, since that's all she cares about.

But one picture, hidden behind the others, is of me and her in Boston a couple of years ago. That was a special vacation for the whole family. Dad wanted to see the old sites back east. It took more than two weeks, mostly in the backseat of the car, where Kathy and I would make the time go by faster by singing, playing games, or fighting.

I pick up the picture and take a good look at Kathy. I bet she's close to the monastery by now.

She doesn't know she's walking into a trap. The least I could do is warn her. She would laugh at me and call me stupid, but at least I would stop her from walking into the monastery. We could throw the bread over the wall and run for our lives.

She would be so thankful to me for saving her life that she would let me choose which CDs I wanted.

She's probably only a block away now.

I throw the picture onto her bed and run down the stairs. Dad drops his paper and looks up at me as I open the front door.

"Mike, where are you going?"

"To get Kathy."

"But you said you were sick."

9
To Kathy's Rescue

The door slams behind me and I jump onto my bike. I pedal faster than I ever have before. I must get to Kathy before she gets inside the monastery. She doesn't understand what's going on up there.

Within a minute I'm at the top of Ash Street. I turn onto Sunset Drive. I don't see Kathy! I'm too late. Kathy has already gone into the monastery.

What do I do now?

I pedal slowly to the iron gate and get off my bike. The courtyard is quiet and dark green. The grass is even longer. Kathy is nowhere to be seen.

I can see that the big wooden door leading into the monastery is open a crack. Kathy must have walked in. Maybe she was dragged in.

I stand by the iron gate, my feet frozen to the sidewalk. Inside that monastery is my sister. By now she knows it wasn't my imagination, but that they really are flesh-eating cannibals. In a way I'm glad. Kathy has always made fun of me and my friends. Now I'll bet she wishes she listened to me.

But she's still my sister, and I've got to try to help

her. I gently push against the gate. It creaks as it opens. The first step into the courtyard is the hardest. My brain tells me to get back onto my bike and get back home. Sisters are replaceable, anyway.

But my thrill side is too excited. Here's my chance to actually go inside the monastery.

Another step.

Perhaps inside there's a row of skulls dangling from ropes. Maybe they have small candles in them, like little lamps.

Step.

Maybe I'll find where the monks roost when they rest. I bet they hang from their feet, upside down.

Step, step.

Maybe they're just using Kathy to get me. Anyone knows that boy meat is better and tastier than girl meat.

Step.

I'm in the middle of the courtyard, standing on the stone steps leading to the big wooden door. I look up at the tower. They must be watching from up there. If they're not asleep.

Step, step, step, step.

I push open the wooden door. It creaks louder than the iron gate, and the echo makes the creak bounce all over the walls inside. I close my eyes and quit breathing.

Listen. Is there anyone moving inside? Is there a monk behind the door trying not to laugh as he waits for me to walk in? Does he have a baseball bat lifted over his head?

I try to look through the crack of the door. It's dark inside. Bad for real people, but good for vampire cannibals.

"She's my sister," I remind myself out loud as I push the door a little bit more, just enough for me to squeeze through. I take my last breath of outside air and walk in.

It's dark and smells funny. I step inside a little further and close the door behind me, but not all the way.

I'm standing in the middle of a hallway with wooden floors. It takes a minute for my eyes to adjust to the darkness. To my left the hallway goes down and turns a corner. Light is coming in from some windows down there.

To my right the hallway disappears into darkness. I think I can see a door at the end of the hall, but I'm not sure.

And the smell. It smells old. Even the museum in town smells better than this.

The light at the end of the hallway looks a lot better than the darkness going the other way. So I turn left and walk toward the light. I take a step, but the wooden floor screams with a loud crack. I freeze, with one foot still in midair, and close my eyes. The creak and crack echo down the hallway and around the corner and probably to a group of hungry monks who wake up with the sound of a young boy walking in their monastery.

I hold my breath, waiting for any sound of footsteps coming from the other side of the hallway. My body's half turned to the door leading outside. I'm still close enough to make my escape.

I think I hear singing. Someone must have a radio on. Nah!

I take another step. The floor creaks again, but not as loud. With each step I get a bit closer to the end of the hallway. The lighter it gets, the better I feel.

I think I hear that singing again.

I get to the end of the hallway. To my right another hallway continues down. Large windows along the hallway let in bright sunlight, and I have to squint to keep from hurting my eyes.

To my left is a large opening into a dark room with stone walls and stone floor. Wooden stairs start at the stone floor and spiral around the walls as they rise. A thick rope dangles in the middle of the room. I tilt my head up to see what the rope is tied to, but it just disappears into the darkness.

The tower!

I'm looking up into the tower. The place where all the cannibal monks live. The wooden stairs must take the cannibal monks up to the top of the tower, where they can look over all of the boys in the neighborhood.

I quickly look down at the floor. I'm afraid that if I look too hard up into the tower, some red glowing eyes will look down at me. Maybe the red eyes have some hypnotic power that will make me climb up the wooden stairs into the darkness where the hungry monks wait.

I back up next to one of the windows letting in light. The warm glow makes me feel safer.

A gust of cold air comes out of the tower and makes my skin shiver. The rope swings back and forth.

Someone must be coming down the rope. It must be the fast way down.

My thrill side looks at the rope. It wants to see who or what is coming down. But now isn't the time to be stupid. I've got to think fast if I'm ever going to get out of here alive.

If I run back to the front door, I've got to run past the tower and into the dark hallway. That would be dumb.

I look down the lighted hallway and see a big double door. Maybe it's a large closet where I can hide.

The rope swings faster and the cold air gets colder.

I run to the middle of the hallway, swing open the double doors, and run inside. I shut the doors behind me and sit on the floor with my back to the doors.

Safe, at least for now.

But I'm not in a closet. I'm at one end of a very large room. In fact, it's enormous. The ceiling goes up at least thirty feet to large wooden beams. It's not dark in the room, but it's not light, either. Pretty colors come in from tall windows along the walls.

Suddenly someone in the room starts singing. I curl up in fright. I'm trapped.

The voice sounds smooth and soft. It doesn't seem like the type of voice that could have a boy for dinner. I slowly stand up and realize that I'm standing in the back of some sort of church, which is full of empty benches.

Are cannibals religious?

At the front of the chapel is the biggest statue of Jesus on the cross I've ever seen. It hangs from the ceiling and almost touches the ground. Two large ropes hold it up. It looks like it's made of wood. It's really colorful.

Just below the statue is a long table with a white tablecloth. A couple of shiny glasses and plates sit on the table.

At the side of the table is the same old monk I saw outside. He's singing as he looks up to the statue. He's sitting in what looks like a large, wooden high chair for a very large baby. But instead of food on his tray, he has a big, old book.

The monk stops singing and reads something from his book. It sounds strange, like a witch's spell. I don't understand a word of it. It's probably some ancient language.

Pratt told me cannibals would burn up if they saw a cross. But the monk is sitting right next to the largest cross I've ever seen. If the cross can burn cannibals, then this one could have exploded more than a million cannibal-vampire monks.

Stupid Pratt.

I stand up a little more to get a better look at the man. It's the same old monk who tried to trap me in the garden and then came to my house.

The monk looks up to the crucifix and starts singing again.

My insides feel like Jell-O and I give out a small moan. My knees start to buckle under me and I begin to sink to the ground.

"Hey, goofy," a voice whispers to me.

It's Kathy! And she's alive!

I stand up straight again and turn around. "You give it to him," Kathy says as she holds the loaf of bread out to me. "He's been standing there singing since I got here." She shoves the bread into my chest. "I'm not waiting around this weird place anymore."

I grab the bread as she walks back out into the hallway.

"No, wait!" I yell, trying to stop her from leaving me alone with the monk. "Come back!"

It's too late. She's left me. I can't believe it. I risk my life to come to her rescue, and she walks out on me.

Stupid sisters.

It's quiet. I don't hear any singing or reading.

I slowly look up. The old monk is still sitting on his high chair, but he's looking at me. I should run, but all I can do is stare at his smile. His evil magic must have worked on my legs. They won't move. He starts walking toward me, then stops and turns around and faces the large statue. He slowly bends on one knee and touches his head and shoulders with his hand, just like a lot of baseball players do before they bat.

I wonder if cannibals know how to play baseball.

As he slowly straightens up, the bones in his knees crack loud enough to echo in the room. He turns back around and walks toward me, his face beaming with that same smile. Behind his smile I can see his dark, yellow teeth. Even though he's smiling, his old teeth worry me.

The monk moves so slow that there's no way he could catch me. All I would have to do is walk away and get out of this monastery. But my stupid legs stand frozen as I watch the ancient man walk to me. Each step he takes gives his face a hint of pain. The effort makes him breathe hard, but his smile remains.

He stops just a few feet in front of me. "Hello, again."

I shove the bread in front of him. "Here, Mom made this for you."

My hand is shaking so bad that I can barely hold up the loaf.

He looks down at the brown loaf and takes it in his hands. He handles it like it was made out of glass.

"It's beautiful," he says as he lifts it up to his nose, closes his eyes, and takes a long smell. "Beautiful."

His smile returns and he pats my arm. "This deserves a celebration," he says as he grabs on to my arm and walks me back out the double doors. "Do you have a name?" he asks as we get out to the hallway.

"Mmm—" I clear my throat. "Mike."

"Hello, Mike. I'm Father Lawrence."

Once out in the hallway, I feel the cool breeze coming from the tower. I don't look directly at the tower, but out of the corner of my eye I can see the rope dangle. But we turn the other way and walk down the hallway, away from the tower. I'm glad he's not going to

79

make me walk up the wooden tower steps to his friends. But I don't feel real good about going deeper into the monastery.

"I've seen you and your friends walking on the back wall a lot. It was just a matter of time before one of you fell."

He looks up at my forehead to see if there are still any scratches. "Are you feeling better?"

I nod my head, still trying to get my tongue and mouth to cooperate.

We get to the end of the hallway and stop. He lowers himself onto one knee and does that baseball thing again.

I look up at the wall and see a small cross hanging by a string on the wall. This place is loaded with the things.

He pulls himself up again, using my arm as a handle. He's heavy enough to almost pull me down to the floor, but I lean hard to the other side until he can grunt his way back up.

He leads me through a door into a room that is pitch-black.

"Wait here; I'll find the switch," he says as he lets go of my arm.

For a few moments I'm standing in this black room, afraid to move. I wonder when all the cannibal monks are going to pounce on me. All I would have to do is turn around and run. But my thrill side wants to see who is in this room. One of these days, my thrill side is going to get me cooked.

I can hear the old monk shuffle around along the wall behind me.

"Ah, here it is," he says.

Click.

The light goes on. I'm standing in the monk's kitchen! There's probably no worse place to be than in the monk's kitchen.

Everything is large. Pots, pans, stoves, refrigerators, cupboards—they all look like a kitchen found in a restaurant, not in a monastery. A boy my size could definitely fit into some of those pots.

I back up to the door, trying to talk sense to my thrill side.

The monk goes to a large butcher block and pulls a huge, gleaming knife out of the wooden block. He places the bread on the table and then holds up the knife.

"Let's take a slice. . . ."

My legs finally wake up. My thrill side has already left the monastery. I'm about to become the main ingredient in a sandwich.

Run! my mind yells to my legs. But I can only walk backward slowly.

"My mom knows I'm up here," I say to the monk.

He looks up at me and smiles as he starts slicing the bread with long strokes of his knife. "That's good," he says as the first piece of bread falls over onto the table. "You must be a good boy to your mother."

I watch as he begins to slice the next piece of bread. His hands are large, with scabs and cracks all over them. They are browner than most hands. I can tell he works with them a lot.

His hands remind me of my grandpa's hands. And Grandpa was the nicest man ever. When he died, we all walked past his open casket. Everyone looked at his face. Except me. I looked at his hands.

I miss those rough hands.

But this isn't Grandpa. This is a monk who has been known to eat boys. And I'm in his kitchen while he is slicing bread for a sandwich with a very sharp knife.

I step back faster and crash out of the kitchen backward. This old monk might have the kind hands of Grandpa, but he's also got a sharp knife and an appetite.

"Wait!" the monk calls out to me as I start down the dark hallway.

I stop for a moment and look back at the kitchen door. The bread sure did smell good. Maybe this monk has given up eating boys. Maybe he just is lonely and wants someone to talk to. Maybe Pratt is wrong.

Maybe he isn't.

I start running down the hall. As I get closer to the tower, the rope swings even faster. They must be coming down to get me before I can escape.

Faster! Faster!

Out of the corner of my eye I see shadows on the wall.

Faster! Faster!

I get to the front door and swing it wide open. With

only a few jumps I'm at the iron gate and outside of the monastery. I grab my bike as I run past it, pulling it with me until I can jump on and ride to the safety of my home.

The old monk may be just an old man with Grandpa's hands.

But maybe he isn't.

10
Pratt's Turn

Pratt doesn't believe me. There's no way he can accept that I went into the monastery and came back out alive.

I tell anyone who will listen about the dark hallway and the rope swinging from the tower. I tell them about the monk's yellow teeth and how he led me into the kitchen. But most of the other kids at school don't believe all the stuff about the monastery, anyway.

Pratt doesn't believe my story, either. "No way!" he says during lunch. "You'd be deep-fried by now."

It has always been assumed that if any boy could survive the monastery, it would be Pratt. He's the bravest and toughest of all the boys in the neighborhood. He also knows the most about the monks in the monastery. It has just seemed likely that if any young boy would have a chance to make it out of the neighborhood alive, it would be him.

I can tell he's hurt that I was the one to finally brave the monastery. He doesn't like anyone to be braver than him.

"If he had a hold of you, he'd never of let you go," Pratt argues.

"What do you know?" I shout back. "You also told us that the sun would evaporate their skin. But you saw the old man walking outside. His skin wasn't even smoking."

"You wouldn't do it again," Pratt says.

"Don't have to. I've already done it twice," I say. "Why don't you go in?"

Pratt just about chokes on his apple. Kenny looks over and waits for Pratt to answer. Kenny would rather drop the whole subject.

"Come to think of it," I say, "you haven't walked the wall in a long time."

"That's because I always win," Pratt protests.

"Maybe you're just scared," I answer back.

Pratt throws his apple as far as he can. He's mad, but he doesn't say anything.

Jenny and Kimberly walk past us.

"Hi, Mike," Jenny says as she smiles at me.

I just nod. Cool people don't have to say anything. All they have to do is nod their heads. And this week, I'm cool.

She doesn't say anything to Pratt, which makes him even madder. He stuffs the rest of his hippo food into his sack and stands up.

"Okay, Cummings," he says. "Today after school I'll walk the wall better and longer than anyone has in the three-thousand-year history of the monastery." He stomps off toward the school. "I'll even dance on the wall," he yells back to Kenny and me.

Kenny is feeling sick. He's probably thinking up some excuse not to go up to the monastery today. He's had enough of the wall in the past couple of weeks.

I just smile and take a bite of my apple.

"We better get in," Kenny says, looking up to the sky. "It's going to rain soon."

I nod my head.

It's a nice ride up Ash Street. Pratt, Kenny, and I take our time. In fact, Pratt is trailing far behind. He's in no hurry. This time it's his turn to walk the wall.

He talked real brave at school, and he knew he would have to do it.

We turn left on Sunset and head for the monastery. Pratt falls further behind. It's been threatening to rain the whole day, but not a drop has come down. The clouds are getting darker and heavier, and thunder can be heard far away. The darkest clouds seem to be hanging over the monastery. The clouds are so dark that they almost look green.

Waiting for us by the wall is a group of younger neighborhood boys. They heard Pratt's bragging in school today and they want to see for themselves this time.

They are the third and fourth graders in the neighborhood. Lately Pratt, Kenny, and I have been telling them the stories of the monastery. We figure that every boy in the neighborhood should know about the dangers he faces. These boys probably have also looked at the tower at night and protected themselves with night-lights and covers.

Now they want to see Pratt walk the wall.

When they see me, they quit talking and stare. They know I'm the one who entered the feared monastery and escaped. I know the secret to survival in this neighborhood.

I smile and nod at them.

Pratt finally rides up around to the wall. His face turns green when he sees all the guys who have come up to watch him walk the wall. For a moment he turns his bike around a bit, like he was about to turn around and race to his house.

But he knows he can't turn back now. He rides the last few feet and jumps off his bike. The boys watching are amazed by his bravery.

Pratt looks up at the wall and puts his hands on his hips. He stands there for a moment, looking like a pirate. He may look real tough and brave, but I know that inside he's worried that the cannibal monks are mad at losing one young boy, and they have no intention of losing another.

He takes a couple of deep breaths, then starts to climb. The third and fourth graders gasp and take a few steps back with their bikes.

I look up at the tower. The green clouds seem to be circling around it. Thunder rumbles in the distance.

This is not a good time to be walking the wall. I feel sorry for Pratt. If it weren't for all the guys watching him, I'd tell him to do it another day. But there's no turning back when you have an audience.

Pratt gets up to the top of the wall and lies on top of it. He's got to be awfully steady today. The wind of the storm is gusting from all different directions and could blow him off into the garden.

The killer roses are bobbing up and down with excitement. They smell boy meat.

Pratt puts one leg under him, then another. He slowly stands as the third and fourth graders ooh and ah. He takes one step, then another. I can see his eyes looking down at the graves.

When he gets to the hungry roses, he stops a moment. He's trying to decide if he should step over the roses or try to walk past them.

Flash.

All of us are blinded by the flash of white light!

Clap!

The sound coming from the tower makes our bones almost leap out of our skins.

Crackle!

Rumble!

Pratt flies off the wall and belly flops onto the ground with a thud. The third and fourth graders scream and climb over one another with their bikes and race away from the monastery. A couple of them even run into me, knocking me off my bike.

Kenny is already halfway down Ash Street, crying.

Pratt has knocked the wind out of himself and tries to gulp down air as he grabs his bike and follows behind the rest of the terrified, screaming boys.

Within seconds I'm left alone—again. The wall still shakes with the thunder's rumble. I look up to the tower.

The bolt must have hit the tower where the dark-green clouds are swirling around.

I think I hear singing. Singing? The old monk must be in his church singing his strange words. He must have some spell that brings swirling green clouds and lightning to his home.

I stand back up and slowly pick up my bike. If I don't make any sudden moves, the cannibals in the tower may not notice me.

I get onto my bike and quietly pedal away. . . .

Flash!

Crash!

I'm halfway down Ash Street.

Crackle!

Rumble! Rumble.

Faster! Faster!

11
Dad Delivers

The storm is loud for most of the night. I lie under my blankets in my lighted room, shaking with each crash and rumble. It's hot under the blankets, but it isn't safe to stick my head out for cool air.

I turn on a small flashlight and look at my watch to check the time. It isn't until after midnight that the storm finally goes away. I can then stick my head out and take a few quick breaths before getting back under the protection of the blanket.

I'm not asleep more than a moment when I hear my door open and somebody walking into my room.

I curl up into a small ball at the bottom of the bed.

"Mike, what's with all the lights?"

It sounds like Dad, but you can never be sure. The cannibal monks could make their voices sound just like Dad's.

Click!

Click!

Click!

Oh, no! Whoever it is just turned off all the lights.

My main source of protection is gone. I crawl further to the bottom of the bed.

"Mike," the Dad voice says, "it's time to get up."

Someone lifts the covers off of me. I hide my face with my hands.

The Dad voice is laughing. "What the—?"

I peek between my fingers. It's still light in the room.

It's morning.

I squint my eyes and look up at my dad. He's looking down at me and laughing.

"You playing a turtle?"

I drop my feet onto the floor. I can't explain it to Dad. He wouldn't believe me, anyway. The way things were last night, he's lucky to have a son anymore. He laughs at my blankets and lights, but he would do the same thing if he were my age.

He plops the covers back down onto my head and walks out of the room.

"I've got something for us to do today," he says. "So get dressed."

I pull the covers off my head and look out the window. The sky is bright blue, without a cloud—except above the monastery, where a small, white cloud is floating over. It's probably the last evil cloud to leave.

I jump into the car. It's usually fun when Dad says he has something for us to do. It might be fishing up on the river or shopping for camping gear downtown.

He backs the car out of the driveway and heads

down the street. But instead of going straight, he turns onto Ash Street and starts going up the hill.

"Where are we going?" I ask.

"I thought we could get your service badge done this weekend."

I have almost all the badges I need to earn my Arrow of Light award. After I get my Arrow, I'll be finished with Cub Scouts. All I have left is to help some old person to get my service badge. Last week Dad and I talked about helping Grandma dig up her garden. But this isn't the way to Grandma's.

At the top of Ash Dad turns onto Sunset Drive, heading toward the monastery.

"Where are we going?" I ask again. This time with more stress.

Dad just smiles. He stops the car in front of the monastery's iron gate. "Here," he says.

"Here?"

Dad's got to be kidding. The only thing I could do for the old monk is feed him—with me!

The Cub Scouts don't expect us to become meals for cannibals. If it did, then no one would be left to become Boy Scouts.

"Last time I went jogging, I noticed that the lawn wasn't being cut," Dad says as he gets out of the car. "I talked to Father Lawrence and said you'd be happy to do it for him." He slams the door shut and waits for me to get out.

Now I wish Dad didn't jog. He does it so that he can stay trim and healthy. But me going back into the monastery won't make me any healthier. Just well-done.

I sit still in the car. Maybe this is just some sort of bad joke Dad is trying to pull on me. He wouldn't really make me go help the cannibal monk. Would he?

"Come on, Mike," he says as he walks to the iron gate.

He's not joking. Dad really is going to make me do this. Maybe the storm did some black magic on him during the night. Maybe he woke up this morning and told Mom, "We need to send Mike up to the monastery." Maybe Mom agreed.

I open the car door and get out. Dad waits for me by the gate.

"After today you'll have all your Arrow badges."

After today I'll be lucky to be alive to get my Arrow.

I trudge over to the gate and wait to be handed over to the monks by my own father. It would be useless to tell him anything. He's probably still mad about the time I sold his set of golf clubs for twenty-five dollars. This must be his way of getting back at me.

"Father Lawrence told me where the mower is," he says as he pushes the gate open.

I follow behind, feeling helpless. If I ran, Dad would just catch me. Then not only would I be eaten by the cannibal monk, but I'd also be grounded for a week.

Dad leaves the stone path and walks over to the side of the monastery. I perk up. Maybe he isn't going to take me inside after all.

We walk across the front courtyard and enter a narrow strip of lawn that is sandwiched between the wall and the monastery. I follow closer behind Dad, putting my feet into the footsteps he makes in the long grass.

The narrow passage opens up into the back garden. I stop and let Dad go ahead. I look up at the tall killer roses, then down to the thirteen graves. Dad keeps on walking. He doesn't worry about anything back here.

Dad must not be too smart.

He stops and turns around. "You coming?" he asks.

"Where are you going?"

He points to the shed. "Over there. Father Lawrence said the mower was in the shed."

Little does Dad know that the shed is used for packing what's left of boys into small caskets.

"Come on, Mike," he says, giving me one of his boy-are-you-weird looks. "You look like you've seen a ghost."

I'm sure I'll see one soon enough around here.

We walk past the graves. The grass on the graves is trimmed neatly. They look like small greens on a golf course.

When we get over to the shed, we stop. Dad fumbles with the latch. I get behind Dad and look down at the ground. My thrill side tries to look up, but I keep my head down.

He swings open the door, and I turn and get ready to run in case anything or anybody flies out of the shed.

"It smells like old, wet tents," Dad says as he looks into the dark shed.

Dad is still alive, so nothing must have jumped out

at him. I turn around and look into the shed. A few garden tools and rakes are neatly hung up along the wall. A couple of bags of fertilizer are on the ground. In the middle is a dark, green lump. It looks like a big cover. Maybe it's covering a body.

Dad walks in while I stay safely outside. That is, if you can call standing in an old cannibal's graveyard safe.

He grabs the cover and lifts it up. I cover my eyes with my hand while my thrill side peeks out between my fingers.

There's no body. Just a strange-looking machine.

Dad starts to laugh. "Mike, you're going to earn this badge."

He pulls the rest of the cover off. I've never seen a machine like it before. It has two wheels about two feet apart. Between the wheels are some curved pieces of metal. A long handle comes up from the wheels and then curves out like bicycle handles about three feet off the ground.

Dad is still laughing.

"What is it?" I ask.

"It's a mower." Dad giggles.

It's not like any mower I've ever seen. There's no grass bag to empty. No gas tank. No motor.

"Where's the motor?" I ask, walking into the shed to get a closer look at this strange mower.

Dad laughs harder. "Right here," he says pointing to my arms. "You're the motor."

I look up at Dad like he's crazy. He made some sort

of joke and is laughing hard at it. But I don't get it.

"It's got to be turned on somewhere," I say. "Maybe it's electric."

Dad grabs the handle and pulls it out of the shed. As he does, the metal blades between the wheels spin.

"Nope. It's not electric," he says as he turns the mower around. "It's manual."

He shoves the mower forward. The blades spin and fling pieces of cut grass into the air. It cuts grass without an engine!

Dad stops. He only went a few feet, but he's breathing hard. He turns around and smiles at me. "I'm too old for this. It's your turn."

I still can't believe that Dad is trying to make me work in the monastery's garden. Especially by the graves. Surely he should know that this isn't the safest place for us to be.

But he stands there holding out the mower's handle to me, waiting for me to try it. I grab the handles and give the mower a push. The blades turn fast, but the long grass stops it cold. I pull it back and get the mower going faster. This time it cuts a couple of feet in the thick, tall grass before it clogs up.

"You serious?" I say as I look up at Dad. "It'll take me all day just to cut ten feet."

Dad pats my shoulders. "It'll make you strong."

"It'll kill me."

He laughs again and gives me a big pat on the back. "Keep at it," he says as he walks toward the front court-yard. "I'll pick you up in about three hours."

I can hear him laughing all the way to the front courtyard and out the iron gate. This must be real funny to him. Leaving me here with a cannibal monk and an ancient mower would pay me back for all his golf clubs I sold.

It won't do me any good to stand around and wait for Dad to come back. He's probably running home and telling Mom to pack up. Within a couple of hours they'll be moved out of the house and on their way to a new town. Away from me and away from the cannibal monks.

I give the mower a big shove. Grass clippings spray up into my face, sticking to the sweat on my forehead. The grass is so long that I have to get running starts and let the mower blades cut until they clog with grass. The rain from last night isn't helping things, either. The grass is heavy and wet, making it hard to slice through.

After a half hour I cut a small path from the back courtyard to the front. I'm tired enough to lie down and take a nap, but I can't slow down. I've got to hurry before Dad packs up everything and drives away with Mom and Kathy.

Besides, the cannibals would love me to fall asleep. I'd never wake up again.

I attack the front courtyard with all that my shoulders, legs, and arms can give. My feet are sore and my hands are bright red. A large blister is starting to grow on my palm.

It's only spring, but the heat feels like mid-July. I'm

about to collapse when the front door of the monastery opens.

I'm too tired to run. Even the old monk could catch me before I was out the front gate.

The monk walks out of the monastery, wearing his same old black robe and carrying a platter. The platter has a large glass of lemonade and a slice of bread with some pink jelly.

"It's time for a break," he says as he walks toward me.

I grab the tall glass of lemonade from the platter and gulp it down. It may be poison. Perhaps a drug to make me sleepy. Maybe it's a special formula that will turn me into a vampire. But it's delicious.

After drinking the whole thing, I put the glass back down on the platter. "Thanks," I say. The monk looks astonished that I could drink so fast.

"I better get you another glass," he says as he places the platter on the grass.

He trudges back up the stone steps and into the monastery. After he goes in, I collapse by the platter. My legs have taken all they can for right now.

I lie on my back and look up at the tower. I think I have it all figured out now. I don't think Father Lawrence could be a cannibal. At least not the main cannibal. His eyes are too nice, and his hands are like Grandpa's.

Maybe he's just the janitor of the monastery, or maybe the monk who is sent out to find the next victim.

But I don't think he could be a cannibal himself. At least not a bad cannibal.

With my thirst taken care of, my stomach starts to growl. I look at the bread with the pink goo on top. It looks strange, but I'm hungry enough to try it.

I pick up the slice, look at it a moment, then take a small bite. It may be jam made from blood, or perhaps from a slime that drips from the monastery walls. Maybe it's a glue that will seal my mouth shut so that I can't scream for help.

But it's delicious.

I take another huge bite. Then another. I never tasted anything like it before. It's sweet and fruity.

When the monk walks out of the monastery holding another tall glass of lemonade, my mouth is full and I'm licking the last of the pink goo off my fingers.

"How was the bread and honey?" he asks.

I stop licking my fingers. "That was honey?" I never cared for honey. The idea of eating bee barf usually makes me sick.

"Cherry whipped honey," he tells me. "It was the last batch we made in 1949."

I look at my fingers in disgust. Not only have I been eating bee barf, but I've been eating very old bee barf.

I wipe my hands on my jeans.

The old monk takes my glass and walks back inside. "I'll be back out in a while with some more lemonade," he says as he walks back into the monastery.

In just under two hours, I've only cut the front courtyard. There's no way I'm going to spend my time cutting around those graves.

My legs finally collapse onto the grass. My fingers and palms ache with blisters. One blister has popped and stings whenever I move my hand. I lie down on the grass and let the sweet smell of cut lawn relax me.

The wooden door creaks open, and out walks the old monk with another tall glass of lemonade and a slice of bread and honey. As slow as he walks, he must have spent all his time walking back and forth from the kitchen.

"Wonderful," the monk says as he looks around the courtyard. He hands me the lemonade and bread. He clasps his hands together as he looks down at the cut lawn. "It hasn't been cut this well for years."

I gulp down the lemonade and chomp into the bread. I close my eyes and enjoy the flavor. It seems to taste even better than the first time.

He waits patiently for me to finish my drink and eat my bread. After I swig my last drop of lemonade and swallow the last bite of the bread, he takes my glass. "Come inside. I've got something for you."

He takes ahold of my arm. At first I want to pull away, but I'm too tired to fight. Together we walk into the monastery.

Instead of turning left and walking toward the tower, we turn right and walk into the darkness. Just a few steps into the hallway, we stop at a door. He opens the door. It's darker in here than in the hallway. He fumbles with his other hand and clicks on a switch. A small yellow light dangling from the ceiling lights up the room.

It's a bedroom, sort of. It has a small bed in one corner of the room. The most surprising thing to me is that he sleeps in a bed, not a casket. Wooden cupboards and a desk go across the opposite wall. A small window looks out to the front courtyard.

A few shelves are loaded with books. All the covers are brown or black. There's not a colorful cover in the whole collection.

He lets go of my arm and walks over to the desk. He pulls open a drawer and pulls out a small box. The box is about half the size of a shoe box. It's made out of leather, with small designs of animals cut into it. On the side it says *Timmy*. It looks like the type of leather work I did with my Cub Scout den when we put our names on some belts.

He gives the dark brown box a smoothing rub with his hand. He treats it like it's made out of glass.

He walks over to the bed and sits down. "Come here," he says as he pats his hand on the bed. I walk over and sit next to him. He carefully opens the box. Inside are hundreds of coins. They are all sizes and colors. He sifts through the coins with his old finger.

"Ah, here it is," he says as he pulls out a small, dark-brown coin. He turns it over and looks at both sides. "You will like this."

He takes my hand and puts the coin in my blistered palm. His rough hand even feels like Grandpa's.

I look down to see a small penny. He's got to be kidding! I work until I'm in pain, and all he gives me is a penny?

"Thanks," I say, pretending I'm satisfied with his cheap payment as I get up off the bed and walk to the door. "I better get going."

He lifts himself off the bed and walks toward me.

"Wait. Can't you stay for a while?" he asks as I head for the front door.

I don't answer. I'm not scared of the old monk anymore. I'm mad. All that work for only a penny!

He gets off the bed and tries to catch up to me. But I get outside before he can even get out of his room. The blisters on my hands make me feel stupid. The sore muscles in my legs make me feel stupid. The stupid mower in the front courtyard makes me feel stupid.

But the old penny in my hand makes me feel the stupidest. If there was a Cub Scout badge for being stupid, I would have earned it today.

"Thank you for helping me today," the old monk says as I get to the front gate. "Please, come and visit me soon."

I turn around and look back at the old, creepy man. I want to throw the penny at him and yell something. But he's standing in the doorway with his hands clasped together, almost like he's saying a prayer. It probably isn't good luck to throw a penny at someone who's praying. I shove the penny into my front pants pocket and stomp out of the monastery.

As I tramp down Ash Street, Dad comes up with the car. He makes a U-turn and stops next to me. I stop and glare at him. He's the one who got me to work for the old monk. He's the one who made me get blisters on my hands. He's the one who made my legs sore.

All for the price of one penny.

For a minute I try to decide if I should get into the car or walk the rest of the way home. That would show Dad. If I walked all the way home, he'd know I was good and mad.

He rolls down the window. "Hey, Mike. Let's go into town for a burger."

I guess I can be just as mad with a hamburger as I could walking home. I stomp over to the car and get in.

"How was it?" Dad asks as he heads toward town.

"Terrible," I growl.

Dad looks over at me. I know he's smiling, but I won't look at him. He thinks it's good for a person to work hard.

"Couldn't be that bad."

I reach down and pull out the old penny. "This is all I got for all that work."

"You weren't supposed to get paid anything," Dad says.

"That's exactly what I got," I say as I hold up the penny so that Dad can see it.

Dad glances at the penny and smiles. "Perhaps Father Lawrence doesn't understand that prices have gone up in the past thirty years."

"It's even old," I complain. I look closely at the date. "1909."

Dad pulls the car over to the curb and stops.

"1909?" he asks as he takes the penny away from me. He looks at the back and front. He holds it closer to him so that he can read the date.

"Maybe we should have a numismatist look at this," he says.

"A what?"

"A coin collector. This penny may be worth something."

He puts the penny into his shirt pocket. If Dad wants the penny so bad, he can keep it. How much could a penny be worth? Especially an old penny.

I'm hungry after all the work I did today, and I want to eat soon. Dad drives into town but he passes our favorite drive-in. He eventually pulls the car up to a small shop with lots of colored paint on the windows that says COINS! BUY! SELL!

There's a lot of other words covering up the windows, all with exclamation points.

When we walk into the store, a little bell above the door jingles. The shop inside isn't much bigger than our living room. A short old man stands behind glass display cases. In the cases are shelves of coins, books about coins, and special holders for coins.

He's talking to another old man, who is looking at some coins.

Dad goes up to the counter. The old man leaves the customer and walks up to us.

"Can I help you?" he says.

"What do you know about this?" Dad asks as he hands the man the penny.

The man gives out a low whistle. Looks carefully at both sides.

"I haven't seen one of these for years," he says as he puts a small magnifying glass in one eye to get a closer look at the penny. "Yep. A 1909 S-VDB."

"An S-VDB?" the other old man says. He drops the coin he was looking at onto the counter and walks over to us.

The shop owner keeps whistling to himself as he looks at the penny. "I'll give you two hundred fifty dollars for it right now," the shopkeeper says.

"Two hundred fifty dollars?" I yell.

"All right. Three hundred dollars, but that's all I can pay this month."

"Are they rare?" Dad asks.

"Quite a few were minted, but for only one year," the shop owner explains. He leans over the counter and points to some very small print right under Abraham Lincoln's head. "See there," he says. Dad leans over and squints his eyes. "It has the initials VDB. That's for Victor D. Brenner, the man who designed the Lincoln penny. His initials only appear on the 1909 series."

"I'll give you three hundred fifty dollars," the customer says.

Three hundred fifty dollars! All of a sudden all the

work I did for that old monk seems worth it. My blister doesn't hurt anymore, and my legs don't ache.

Dad takes the coin from the dealer. "No. I think we'll keep it. It's from a friend."

I can't believe what I'm hearing. I earned the penny, and now Dad won't let me sell it. A penny for 350 dollars! That comes out to about 100 dollars an hour. I could buy the best bike in the neighborhood and still have some money left to get some new video games.

"That's some friend," the shop owner says.

I'm so mad I feel my face burn red. It wasn't a friend. It was an old, creepy monk who needed his lawn cut.

Instead of selling the penny, Dad buys a book about coins and a special type of folder to put coins in.

When we get back into the car, I'm still too mad to talk. Dad gives me back my hard-earned penny.

"Father Lawrence must like you very much to give you that," Dad says. "It's something you can hang on to until you really need the money."

He starts the car and drives away from the coin shop. I look down at the old, brown penny.

A gift from a friend? Dad has got to be kidding!

I lie in bed and read the coin book Dad bought for me today. My body aches from all the mowing I did for the old monk. Actually, it feels good to be so tired. I open my hand and look at the penny for the millionth time today.

I roll over and look out my window. The stone tower glows from the moonlight. There are no bats swooping out of the tower. No glowing eyes. Only an old monk who is too weak to mow his own lawn.

I roll over and turn off my light.

12
Father Lawrence's Work

Get up, Mike." Someone is talking in my dream.

A hand nudges my shoulder.

"Get up." It's that stupid voice again. It's low and quiet. It almost sounds like my dad.

The hand nudges me again. This time my brain lets go of my dream and decides it's time to see who is trying to wake me up.

The light coming from my window makes it hard for me to open my eyes more than a billionth of a millimeter. But between the tiny slits my eyelids make, I can see the smiling, fuzzy face of Dad.

It must be Saturday. Dad never shaves on Saturday. He says he likes to give his old face a day off, too, during the weekends.

I close my eyes, hoping he'll go away.

"Come on, Mike. We've got to get up to the monastery."

We? Dad was the one with the great idea of cutting the old monk's lawn every weekend. Why doesn't he cut it himself?

I roll over and groan.

"I'll get you some breakfast ready," Dad says as he walks out of the room.

I drop one leg onto the floor. I can hear a thud, but I can't feel much. My brain is still trying to change from dreaming to waking.

I roll over, drop the other foot onto the floor, and slowly sit up. I have a severe case of morning pain. My eyes hurt, my skin feels tight, all the joints in all my bones are frozen in some sort of overnight liquid.

I hurt. I always do if I wake up before seven.

I look over to the clock. Six-thirty.

"We?" I mumble as I stand up.

Pratt and Kenny wanted me to meet them in the park before our baseball practice begins.

They think I'm crazy to mow the monk's lawn. They think the cannibals are just waiting for me to get bigger before they eat me.

Dad drives "us" to the monastery, but only I get out of the car.

"I'll pick you up in two hours," Dad says as he drives off.

"We" have to finish mowing the lawn in time for "our" baseball practice.

I walk up to the gate and swing it open. For the first time, the loud creak doesn't make me jump in fear, but I still don't trust the old monk completely.

The singing of birds from just about every tree greets me.

I walk through the front courtyard and onto the narrow strip of lawn, heading toward the back garden. As the narrow strip widens in the back where the garden is, I see the old monk kneeling by the graves. I stop and watch.

It looks like he's praying, but I hear a snipping sound, like a pair of scissors. I look closer at the old monk and realize that he's clipping the grass on the graves. The lawn has grown up in the week I haven't been here, but the graves are groomed to perfection.

The so-called lawn mower is at the end of a small cut path. It looks like someone has tried unsuccessfully to cut some of the tall grass.

"Father Lawrence?" I quietly say.

The old monk turns around. Sweat is pouring from his forehead. Even clipping some blades of grass is too hard for this old man, but he does it anyway.

His yellow teeth gleam as he smiles. "Hello, Mike." He starts to get up, but not with much success. I walk over to him and take his arm. Leaning on me, he finally stands.

"We—ah—I thought I'd mow your lawn again," I say.

He looks at the lawn mower. "I tried to do it myself yesterday," he says. "I'm afraid it's too big a job for you."

"No problem," I answer, feeling powerful. "It'll only take me a couple of hours."

"Well," he says. "I'll get some lemonade made for us."

He walks into the monastery from the back door. After the door shuts behind him, I grab the handle of the mower and pull it back. With a mighty shove, I push it through the tall grass, making a small pathway.

This time I finish the back courtyard before going to the front. When I get to the front, Father Lawrence walks out with a plate that has two slices of bread.

He continues to bring out lemonade and slices of bread as I work. In less than two hours, I finish with the back and front. After the last blade of grass is cut, I lean on the mowing machine.

As I catch my breath, I hear the sound of birds. It seems like each tree is a home for a different bird. They like to sing to one another. For the first time I notice that the walls tend to cut out all noise from the outside. A car driving by sounds like it is far away.

It's a nice kind of quiet. You can even hear the breeze through the birds' nests.

I push the lawn mower to the back courtyard, but stop when I see Father Lawrence clipping away again on the graves. I leave the lawn mower and walk up to him.

"Who are they?" I ask quietly, making sure I don't startle him.

Father Lawrence stops clipping. He turns around and sits on the ground. "My brothers," he says very quietly.

He pats the mound of grass where he has been clipping. "This is Father Thomas. He was the brother who made the honey."

He then points to a couple of graves down. "That's Father Amos. He would trim the trees in the courtyard and take care of birds with broken wings."

He starts clipping Father Thomas's grave again. "I'm

just making sure they have a peaceful rest. It's just part of my work."

I sit down next to him. Not so much that I care to listen to him, but because I'm tired.

"You get paid to do this?" I ask.

"Not with money," he says. "But no one is richer than I."

"Were you always a monk?"

He stops clipping again. This time he puts down the shears and looks up to the skies.

"No. I started out a soldier."

A soldier? Father Lawrence a soldier? I just can't picture this old man dressed up like G.I. Joe and shooting a rifle. Now I'm interested.

"You mean, like an army soldier, with a gun and everything?" I wonder out loud.

"Yes, with a gun and everything." He smiles. "I left Newark in 1930 when I was sixteen and joined up with the meanest bunch of marines you ever knew."

This guy really used to be G.I. Joe.

"When World War II came around, they placed me with an engineering division, where I drove big bull-dozers to make roads for our tanks and soldiers."

He clears his throat and tries to keep the tears in his red eyes.

"We were at Dachau toward the end of the war. My company was building bridges over small streams so that the tanks and troops could hurry into Munich."

He pats the grave next to him, almost like he doesn't

want to bother the graves with such disturbing thoughts.

"My sergeant told me to take my bulldozer to a concentration camp nearby. As I got closer to the camp, I could smell death. They didn't need my bulldozer to make a road or a bridge. They needed the blade to push hundreds of dead bodies into huge pits."

He wipes his eyes and pulls out a handkerchief. It looks like the same handkerchief he gave me when I fell off the wall. He wipes his nose with it.

"At first I didn't think much of it. It was war, and a lot of people got killed. But as the blade pushed the bodies to the pit, an arm or leg would roll up over the blade. Once in a while a head would pop up and stare at me. It was then that I knew my job in life was praying for people."

"That's a job?" I ask.

"Yes. And an important one, too."

He coughs out his emotion and clears his throat. "I joined a monastery right after the war and was eventually sent out here in 1948."

He struggles to stand up. With a few grunts and groans, he gets off the ground.

"It was a beautiful place. Full of hay fields, beehives, and orchards. We had a small herd of cows for milking.

"Pretty soon little housing developments started to spring up outside of town, getting closer to us."

"What happened?"

"We all got old. Too old to haul hay, make honey, and

milk cows. I was actually the last to join the monastery. Eventually we had to sell the land so that we could keep the monastery and continue to pray."

He looks down at the graves. "And they are all at rest." He coughs again and wipes his eyes. "But who's going to bury me?" he says quietly.

He takes my arm and walks me to the back door. "And what about you?" he says cheerfully. "How are we going to repay you for such a good job?"

I feel funny getting paid for mowing the lawn this time. I did it for a friend. "Nothing," I say. "You've paid me enough."

Father Lawrence smiles. "Ah, so you found out about the penny?"

"Yeah. Did you know it was worth three hundred dollars?"

"Three hundred dollars," he says excitedly. "A lot of money for a penny." He stops me and looks at me with a twinkle in his eyes. "Did you sell it?"

I pull the penny out of my pocket. "No. It's right here." I hold it up for him. "Do you want it back?"

He pushes my hand down and grins. "No. No. You earned it."

13
Eleven Years Old

It finally came! The birthday all boys in the neighborhood wait for.

Today I'm eleven years old. It is supposed to be the most important birthday in my life. It used to mean that I would no longer be hunted by the cannibal monks.

But for the past month or two, I haven't been that worried. At some time, maybe thousands of years ago, the monastery may have been the castle of boy-eating monks. But for the last fifty years it's just been the home of Father Lawrence and his buddies.

And he doesn't even eat meat.

In fact, he even gave me an 1898 Indian-head penny for my birthday.

This is an "odd" year, so I couldn't have a huge party. On all my "even" birthdays, I get to have as many friends as I want for a party. But on odd years, Mom and Dad want me to have just a family party. They tell me it's good to just have the family celebrate once in a while. But I think they just don't want all the noise from my friends.

With a little begging, they let me have Pratt and Kenny for an overnighter. We stay up late, telling one another scary stories. The idea is to tell a story so scary that none of us will want to sleep.

It used to be that all the scary stories were about the monastery and its flying monks. But a lot of the fear of the monastery went away after Pratt and Kenny knew I could go in and out of the monastery without being eaten.

"What's in the tower?" Kenny asks.

"I don't know," I say. I'm a bit ashamed. I still don't have the courage to see what's at the top of the tower. I've walked by it many times, but I don't even like to look up when I pass it. It still seems evil.

Pratt gets a gleam in his eyes. "Coffins," he says.

Kenny gets a little lower in his sleeping bag.

"No way," I answer. "Probably nothing."

"There's only one way to find out," Pratt says.

I look over to Pratt. He has a big grin on his face. He knows he's got me now. Everybody in the neighborhood thinks I'm the bravest person in the world. But Pratt can't wait to tell everybody that I'm too chicken to climb up the tower.

"I'll go up it if you guys come with me," I say.

Kenny crawls into a little lump at the bottom of his bag. Even Pratt sinks lower, so only his eyes are poking out. He's not smiling anymore.

"I'm not eleven yet," he says quietly. "It wouldn't be safe for me."

Pratt's right. If I was him, I wouldn't go up there, either. Father Lawrence may be a kind, softhearted vegetarian, but who knows what's up in the tower?

There's only one way to find out.

14
In the Tower

It was supposed to be a nice, lazy summer, but Dad keeps dragging "us" up to the monastery to mow Father Lawrence's lawn. However, it always seems to be me who does all the work. The lawn mower is still hard to push, but my arms seem to be growing bigger each week.

Sometimes I'll stand in front of the mirror in my room and flex my muscles. I think I've even gotten bigger than Pratt.

Pratt and Kenny still refuse to walk into the courtyard. Most of their time is spent watching me from the wall and waiting for me to finish so that we can play at the park.

I'm getting quite a collection of coins now. Every time I get a coin from Father Lawrence, I check it in my coin books and read about it. The coin dealer in town gets excited to see me every time I come in. He wants to see the latest coin. Almost every coin he wants to buy.

Mom sends me up to the monastery with a loaf of

bread each week. Sometimes I have to wait in the chapel until Father Lawrence finishes his praying and singing. His work.

One Saturday in August I decide I'm finally tired of mowing Father Lawrence's lawn with his push mower. I can do the job faster and easier with Dad's mower.

I push the mower up to the monastery. It's hard, but not as hard as mowing a big lawn with caveman technology.

I swing open the gate and push Dad's mower inside. With one pull I get the modern machine screaming and ready to eat any grass that gets in its way. The birds are startled by the engine and fly off to find a quieter spot. I push the bar on the handle and let the machine pull me through the grass with little effort.

Father Lawrence comes running out of the monastery, waving his arms. He's not smiling and seems upset. His mouth is moving, but I can't hear him over the noise of the lawn mower.

I've never seen Father Lawrence move so fast. I pull the throttle back and the machine putters to a stop.

". . . must stop that!" Father Lawrence screams. When he realizes that the engine is stopped, he takes a deep breath. It's almost like he's counting to ten so that he won't hit me.

The red in his face finally fades, and he opens his eyes. "Mike, you must not use that machine here," he says quietly but firmly. "God speaks in whispers, not yells. And if I'm to talk to God, I must be able to hear him."

I look down at the mower, the infernal machine of noise. I may have caused God to fly off with the birds to a quieter place.

Father Lawrence sees that he may have yelled at me a little too harshly. He puts his comforting hand on my shoulder. "The beginning of wisdom is silence," he says gently. "That's the problem with the world today. Everything is loud. No one can hear God anymore. My work must have silence."

I notice a few birds coming back to their trees. I feel better.

"It's time for a snack," he says as he pulls me away from Dad's satanic mower. "Let's go inside for a while."

Once inside the monastery, I feel almost afraid to speak. Maybe God is mad at me for making too much noise. I'm afraid that if he comes back now to talk to Father Lawrence, he might see me here and do something to me—perhaps glue my mouth shut.

But Father Lawrence's hand reassures me. At least God won't hurt me now, especially since I'm holding up Father Lawrence.

As we pass by the tower, the wind blows down through and the rope sways widely. We pass by in silence, but my eyes look up the spiral stairs that lead into the darkness in the tower.

The snack in the kitchen is the usual bread and honey, along with some carrot sticks. I've started to notice that Father Lawrence eats only bland food. Even the honey gets old after a while. I don't see how eating only vegetables and fruits can make it easier for a person to talk to God.

"Ever had pizza?" I ask, thinking he's been in this place so long that he wouldn't know what good food is. Even God must like pizza.

"I make one of the best pizzas in town," he answers. "Mushrooms, onions, green peppers, with a layer of melted mozzarella."

"No pepperoni or sausage?"

He shakes his head. "Meat is not for the person who needs to talk to God for a living."

"You've got to be kidding," I say. "What about Big Macs, Whoppers, Quarter Pounders?"

"What are those?"

I sit on a stool, too amazed to answer. This man must have been frozen a thousand years ago, before food was discovered. I always thought that the basic four food groups were meat, fruit, milk, and the white stuff found inside Twinkies. Father Lawrence doesn't even know what a Twinkie is!

Only a few months ago I thought this was the castle of cannibal, boy-eating, vampire monks. But it ends up that there is only one old man in this castle, and he doesn't even know what a Big Mac is!

Not even Pratt would believe this story.

"I better get going with the lawn," I say as I grab my slice of meatless bread and honey and walk out of the kitchen. Our baseball team is in the summer tournament, and I've already been late for games because of Father Lawrence's lawn.

But when I get to the tower I slow down. I remember what Pratt said on my birthday.

There's only one way to find out what's at the top.

I walk closer to where the wood of the hallway turns into the stone of the tower. I finish the last bite of my bread and lean backward, looking up as far as I can into the tower.

The rope goes through a hole in a wooden ceiling far up in the tower. The stairs also mysteriously stop at the ceiling. There must be something beyond the ceiling. And my thrill side has waited long enough. It wants to know now.

I look behind me to make sure that Father Lawrence is not watching. Sure that I'm alone, I step out of the wood hallway, onto the stone floor. A gust of cold air seems to pour on me from above, making my skin tighten. I step onto the first wooden stair. It creaks louder than anything in this monastery, and that means it's the loudest creak in the world.

If there's anyone up in the tower, they know I'm coming.

I hold my breath for a while and wait to hear if Father Lawrence is coming to find out what the creak was. I'm not sure why, but I feel that Father Lawrence doesn't want me going up here. Perhaps the secret of the entire monastery is hidden above the wooden ceiling.

I step up another stair. My tennis shoe leaves a distinct pattern in the thick layer of dust covering the stairs.

Creak by creak, I make my way to the ceiling. I must be more than twenty feet from the stone floor below.

Finally I can go no more. The wooden ceiling just stops the stairs from going any further. There's a door in the ceiling with a small latch. I look down for one last time, click open the latch, and push open the door.

Cool air rushes down on me from the door. The stairs go through the door and into a small room. But this room isn't like any of the other rooms in the monastery. It's full of sunlight. On each side of the room are three tall slits. They're like windows, but with no glass in them.

In the middle of the room is a bell that is bigger than me. The rope is tied to a big wheel attached to the bell. The rope goes through the floor and down toward the bottom of the tower. The floor and bell are covered with white bird droppings.

Best of all, there're no coffins. Pratt's wrong again.

I look out each side of the tower. It's beautiful. I'm in the highest spot of the highest thing in our neighborhood. I can see every house, even my bedroom window. Pratt was at least partially right: If there were cannibal monks watching from up here, they would be able to watch every boy in the neighborhood.

For the next half hour I look at every house in the neighborhood and every person I can see. It all looks so much different from up here.

After a while, I finally turn around and look at the

bell. Two big arms hold the bell up off the floor. If it was to swing, the bell would hit me in the knees.

I kneel down and look inside the bell. A large metal ball at the end of a rod dangles from the center. I reach in and move the ball. It seems to swing freely. I wonder why I've never heard the bell since I lived in the neighborhood.

I stand back up and grab the big wheel attached to the rope. It squeaks as it moves.

Clang!

I fall backward onto the floor. The clang echoes in my head.

Now I'm in trouble. If God didn't like the lawn mower, he's never coming back after that noise.

I hear a muffled voice down at the bottom of the tower. "Mike?"

I crawl over to the open door in the floor and lie on my stomach. I can see Father Lawrence looking up the tower at me. He doesn't seem too happy.

"Just me, Father Lawrence," I yell down.

"Get down right away. You might get hurt."

My ears tell me that getting away from the bell would be a good idea. One more clang like that just might split my head.

I swing over to the stairs and walk down, closing the door behind me. The clang has made me a bit dizzy, and I have to lean on the stone wall as I go around the tower. When I get to Father Lawrence, I see a look of concern, not anger.

"You must be careful," he says, brushing bird mess

and dust from my shirt. "You could get hurt on those steps."

I look back up the tower. "What's the bell for?"

He takes my arm as we walk to the front door. "It was for the *Opus Dei.*"

"What's the *Opus Dei*?"

"The Work of God. Long before you were even born, the bell would ring seven times a day to have us come in for prayer and singing."

"I never heard it ring," I say while he stops at a cross on the wall and does his standard kneeling.

He chuckles as he pulls himself up. "That rope would go up and down five or six feet. It was all you could do to hang on the end of the rope and swing with it. Father Amos was the last one strong enough to hold on. He would look like a black parachute each time he would come down.

"When Father Amos died, there was no one strong enough to ring the bell," he says, turning his chuckle to a sad sigh. "Pity. Christmas morning was never the same without the ringing. Father Amos would hang on for almost twenty minutes."

He walks me back outside and tells about the days when they were all younger. But I can't hear every word. The bell is still echoing in my head.

I go back to mowing the lawn, with Father Lawrence's hard-to-push-but-quiet mower. The birds are back in the trees, and God must be back on speaking terms with Father Lawrence.

But the clang stays in my ears.

15
The Bell

Our PTA has a big back-to-school fair the first week in September. I win first prize at the school fair for my large collection of rare and old coins.

Everyone stops by to take a look at the coins from the cannibal monk. They lean over the table and get close looks at the bronze, copper, and silver pieces of metal. But no one dares touch any of them. Pratt tells everyone in the school that if someone touches the coins, a special black-magic spell will come over them and they will walk like a zombie into the cannibal castle.

As usual, Pratt doesn't know what he's talking about, but I don't care. It gets everyone excited enough to come look at my magical coins.

Mrs. Liffreth, our principal, looks at every one of the coins carefully. Each coin gets her own deep whistle or an "Oh, my." She tells me she was a coin collector for many years, but has never seen such a unique collection. She even offers me twenty dollars for one of my Indian-head quarters.

"Not for sale," I proudly state. I worked hard for these coins and I'm not about to sell one of them. Not even my 1943 zinc penny, which isn't worth more than fifty cents. I wouldn't even give Jenny Wilson one of my coins.

Now that school's in, and the weather is cooler, I can spend more of my Saturdays watching cartoons instead of mowing Father Lawrence's lawn. But once in a while, I still ride my bike up to the monastery and look out over the neighborhood from the tower.

Some Sundays Mom lets me go up and listen to Father Lawrence sing instead of going to our church. I'm not real thrilled to sit in the chapel, but Father Lawrence's service is much shorter than our church's.

Father Lawrence doesn't have more than ten or twenty songs, so I've gotten to know each one. I don't understand the words, but I can hum right along.

He seems to be getting slower than usual lately. Perhaps the cold weather makes his old bones harder to move. Ever since October, he's been walking like a dinosaur. And the monastery never seems to warm up. Father Lawrence says there's a furnace in the basement, but it doesn't work very well. He bundles up in a thicker robe and goes about his work of praying and singing.

When the cold weather first came, he started to get a bad cough. His singing got choppy as coughs cut up the songs into small pieces.

But, as always, Mom's homemade bread seemed to make even his worst day of hacking and coughing more enjoyable.

Mom wanted him to come to our house for Thanksgiving, but he told me that he was going to spend the entire day thanking God. So Mom has me take up an entire picnic basket of candied yams, pumpkin pie, salad, and anything else Father Lawrence can eat. Of course, turkey is not allowed.

Together we eat in the large monastery dining hall. At one time, the hall could seat at least fifty monks. Now it's only me and Father Lawrence as we eat at the end of the hall, beneath a large painting of Jesus.

Father Lawrence has to stop throughout our meal to cough. Not just a simple cough, but a series of coughs that take him more than a minute to get over. With each coughing fit, his face turns to a light blue.

Anytime I mention his coughing, he just waves his arm. "The cold weather always does this to me."

"What has the doctor said about it?" I ask.

"No need for a doctor. I haven't seen one in twenty-five years and I've been just fine." Cough, cough.

I don't bring up the subject anymore. A man as old as Father Lawrence must have some idea what his body needs and doesn't need.

We spend the rest of our Thanksgiving meal talking about girls, being young, and stuff like that. He tells me of his dates when he was young, and I tell him about my secret love for Jenny.

Surprisingly, for a man who hasn't touched a girl for almost fifty years, he knows quite a bit about women.

He coughs for another solid minute.

"You know," I say, "I bet you'd have more fun if you got another monk to live with you."

He laughs a bit, mixed in with his coughing. "I have plenty of company. Besides, there are no more of my order. I'm the last relic. When I'm gone, the Church will sell the monastery."

"To who?"

"Probably some restaurant or fancy wedding place."

If the restaurant knew the reputation of this place, they'd never consider buying it.

Father Lawrence looks down at his watch. "I better get back to work."

He stands up and leans over to give me a hug. "Tell your mother thank you very much. She is such a good cook." He starts to clean up our dishes.

"I'll take care of these," I say as I pick up the dishes from the table.

"Bless you, Michael," he says with his hands clasped together in front of him. He walks out as I finish the cleaning.

I watched the news last night and decided that Father Lawrence's work just might be important. He shouldn't waste time cleaning dishes when there are famines to stop, murderers to catch, and drugs to destroy. And while he's at it, he could ask God to help that boy on the news who was beaten by his father. Dishes just don't seem that important when all that is going on in the world. Father Lawrence is going to have to work overtime to solve all of these problems.

I stack all the dishes and take them into the kitchen. After filling the sink with hot water, I open the counter below the sink for the soap.

Next to the soap is an old glass bottle with some brown liquid. I pull it out. The label is old and brown. *Klasik Kleaner.* It's some sort of tarnish remover, the same stuff Mom uses to clean her silverware.

But the monastery doesn't have any silverware, just a . . .

A bell.

I walk past the chapel with my rags, brushes, pail of soapy water, and the bottle of Klasik Kleaner. Inside I can hear Father Lawrence singing out his work, mixed in with some coughs.

I walk up the winding stairs of the tower and open the door of the bell room. Once at the top, I close the door quietly. Even though I come up here a lot, Father Lawrence would still be worried.

The bell is covered with years' worth of bird mess and dirt. I have to walk down and replace my soapy water three times. But eventually I get off the years of gunk.

I pour some of the Klasik Kleaner onto one of the dry rags and rub it onto the bell. The light-brown liquid immediately turns into a black goo.

I take another rag and rub off the goo.

Underneath the grime and goo is a bright, silvery bell. It reflects the sunlight like a mirror.

★ ★ ★

It's a project that takes almost a month. I quietly go up into the tower to clean the bell while Father Lawrence goes on with his work.

And I don't just stop with the bell. I clean the entire room. It soon becomes my favorite place to be in the whole world. I can look out of the tower and see everything going on in the neighborhood. It's like I know everything going on.

Around two o'clock, the sun hits the bell just right, and the entire room lights up like a million light bulbs were turned on in the room.

16
The Search

Just about done. Almost everyone on my list has something for Christmas.

I've gotten Mom a purple scarf and Dad a carved smoking pipe. He doesn't smoke, but it's a neat-looking pipe, anyway.

I bought Kathy a big chocolate bar, but I already ate half of it.

Kenny and Pratt are getting the latest comic book series of Batman. That is, if I finish them before Christmas.

But what about Father Lawrence? There's nothing I could buy him that he would need.

I can't buy him a videotape or a video game. He's never even seen a TV. And clothes are definitely out. He only wears his old black robe.

Comic books are no good. I've only seen him read from the big book in the chapel. He says he doesn't even want to read the newspaper.

Knee pads! That would be great. He's always kneeling down and talking to God. You'd think he'd run out of things to say, but he always comes up with something.

But if Father Lawrence won't wear tennis shoes for comfort, he's surely not going to be putting on some knee pads.

What would an old monk like for Christmas?

17
The Gift

I've never found it hard to wake up Christmas morning, but five-thirty is a bit too early even for me. But my gift to Father Lawrence has to be given very early to be any good.

My plan has to be timed perfectly to work. I figure it will be another hour before my sister wakes up, so I have plenty of time.

It must have snowed last night. New flakes have gathered on my window. This wouldn't be a good day to ride my bike, so I better put on my boots along with my heavy coat and snow pants.

I walk quietly past Kathy's door and down the stairs. Compared to the squeaking wood floors and stairs of the monastery, our house is quiet.

It's the coldest day of the year as I tread up Ash Street through the new snow. The neighborhood remains dark. Hopefully, no one is getting out of bed yet.

My feet slip on the snow, making it slow going up Ash. But I finally make it to the top, huffing out big clouds of breath into the cold, dark air.

I turn onto Sunset and head for the monastery.

I push open the iron gate and walk into the court-yard. The birds don't greet me anymore. They left a few months ago. But the wind still whistles quietly through the branches.

My footprints are the only things to mess up the beautiful white courtyard as I walk up to the front door.

I slowly open the door and poke my head in. I hold my breath. From the chapel comes a quiet singing voice, along with the few cough spasms.

Father Lawrence and I are the only ones awake this Christmas morning. He's busy at work singing to God.

I'm busy at work giving my gift.

I walk quietly to the bell tower. It seems as cold in the monastery as it does outside.

The singing from the chapel seems different. A bit lighter and happier than most days. In fact, it's not a song I'm familiar with, and I thought I knew them all. God must enjoy hearing different music on Christmas morning.

I walk up the tower stairs and into the bell room. I want to take a long look outside in the darkness. Only the streetlights can be seen reflecting off the bright white snow. I can see my footsteps on the sidewalk coming up Ash Street.

No Christmas lights have been turned on yet. That's a good sign. No one is awake yet. My gift will be the first thing the entire neighborhood will receive.

I walk back down the steps until I'm about five feet above the stone floor.

I check my gloves on my hands. They seem secure. I look at my watch. 5:53.

"Merry Christmas, Father Lawrence," I whisper. After a moment of hesitation, I jump off the stairs and grab the rope.

I pull the rope down with me.

Clang!

My feet barely touch the ground as the rope jerks me back up the tower.

Clang!

Down.

Clang!

Up.

Clang!

All I have to do is give a small push off with my feet when they reach the floor—

Clang!

—and the rope jerks me back up again.

Clang!

It's all I can do to hang on to the rope. The bell seems to be alive and happy as it rings out for all the neighborhood.

Clang!

I'm spinning around the rope as I go up and down. My plan was to ring for a half hour, but I'm not sure I can make it. The bell's swing makes my arms tired and heavy.

But if Father Lawrence can pray for the people starving in Africa, then I can hold on for another twenty minutes.

Finally, my arms can't take any more, and I let go of the rope. I fall to the floor and lie on my back on the cold stone. The rope above me is still moving up and down and swaying back and forth.

Clang!

The bell wants to live on, but its last sound is a . . . *clang*.

I look at my watch. 6:36. More than a half hour!

I stand up and run up the stairs. I look out the windows of the tower. Every house in the neighborhood has its lights on. Green, blue, red, and yellow lights blink on trees, bushes, and houses.

Through the still-dark sky I can see people standing in their front yards looking up to the bell tower. Other families are looking out their windows. I can even see one or two people walking up Ash Street.

My spine goes cold. What if they are coming to complain? What if they are going to take me and give me to the police?

I look closer at the people walking up the street. They are holding hands and walking slowly. They don't look like a group of people trying to get the kid who woke them up. At least I hope they don't.

I run down the stairs and down the hall. The best part of giving a gift is seeing the person smile. And I can't wait to see Father Lawrence's smile.

I open the doors of the chapel. Father Lawrence is sitting on his chair. I don't want to bother him, so I wait at the back of the chapel.

Maybe he didn't hear the bell in here. I feel a bit disappointed. But I look a little closer at him and see a small smile.

He's breathing hard and his smiling face is white. "Beautiful," he says in a whisper. He starts one of his coughing spells, lasting almost a minute. Each cough sounds harder and deeper.

At the end of his coughing he gulps a big breath of air. His face has turned almost blue, but he's still smiling. "Beautiful."

One of his hands falls from the book and hangs at his side. That's unusual. He always prays with his hands together.

Something isn't right.

I walk out quietly, leaving him in his cold chapel.

I can hear Jenny and her family laughing and talking as I walk up the steps to their front door. They must be unwrapping some of their presents. Jenny's dad is a doctor, so she must have a lot of presents to open.

I push the doorbell. The talking and laughing stop and the door opens. It's Jenny.

"Hi, Mike," she says to me, smiling.

"Is your dad home?" I ask.

"Sure." She opens the door a bit wider. "Come on in."

I step inside, and she closes the door behind me.

"Dad," she yells. "It's for you."

"Did you hear the bells this morning?" she asks. "They were real pretty."

I nod my head.

Jenny's dad walks in. "Merry Christmas, Mike."

"Father Lawrence needs help," I blurt out. I can feel my face turn red and my eyes water. I'm a bit embarrassed for Jenny to see me cry, so I look down at my feet.

"I'll get my bag," he says. "Why don't you get into the car, and we'll drive up and take a look at him."

He goes upstairs and leaves Jenny and me together. I wipe my eyes but don't look up. Jenny must think I'm a real sissy.

"Dad says you help that old man out a lot," she says quietly. "I think that's real nice."

I just nod, watching the snow melt on my boots.

Father Lawrence only lasted a week longer. Jenny's dad told me that it was a massive heart attack. Apparently Father Lawrence had been fighting a bad case of pneumonia, and it made his heart real weak.

Father Lawrence prayed for everybody.

But who prayed for him?

18
The Cannibal Nuns of Sunset Drive

The rest of the winter goes by too slow. I can't remember it being so cold before. Maybe Father Lawrence also prayed for good weather. Without Father Lawrence, maybe the whole world will be covered by snow.

And the evening news seems to be getting worse. More drugs, more murder. We really need Father Lawrence now.

It's been three months since Father Lawrence died. The monastery looks even colder and uglier than before. The tower still rises up and looks over the neighborhood, but there's no one to look out of it.

It's also been three months since I was at the monastery. I was invited to the funeral by Father Francis, a priest from the big cathedral downtown. Father Lawrence's coffin was put into a grave next to the other buried monks. A new stone marker that says FATHER TIMOTHY LAWRENCE was placed on top of the grave.

Father Lawrence took such good care of the thirteen graves. But no one is there to take care of his.

* * *

We get off our bikes and walk over to the wall. It's been so long since Pratt, Kenny, and I climbed the wall that we're not sure we can do it again. But our feet remember, and they push us up to the top. The stones in the wall feel warm on my face as I lie down and look at the garden below.

The snow has melted and left a soggy, dead garden behind. Father Lawrence's grave lies at the end of the others. I'm not sure what I should do to take care of his grave, but I feel I should try something.

I spin around on my stomach and drop into the garden. It's just me and the fourteen monks sleeping in their graves.

Pratt and Kenny stay up on the wall. They still aren't real sure about the monastery. Pratt doesn't say much about cannibals and bats anymore, but he still won't go beyond the wall.

I walk over to Father Lawrence's grave and kneel down. I used to find Father Lawrence kneeling by the graves a lot. He said he liked to talk to his old friends.

I put my hand on the mound of dirt covering Father Lawrence. "Hi," I say as I pat the dirt gently. I'm not too sure what you say to someone who's dead.

"Hello?"

Someone answered!

Father Lawrence never told me that his old friends would talk back to him! I jump up and run backward. I don't know a lot about dead people, but I don't think you're supposed to hear them talk.

Pratt and Kenny give a small scream as they jump down onto the other side of the wall and ride away to safety on their bikes.

I think it's time to get some new friends.

A hand grabs my shoulder. My body doesn't know what to do. Run? Scream? If the person holding me is someone who came back from the dead, then there's little my body could do to escape.

My knees buckle and I crumble to the ground in a scared heap.

"You must be Michael?" a voice says behind me. It isn't Father Lawrence's voice, though. It's soft and gentle. It sort of sounds like my grandmother.

I look at the hand on my shoulder. It isn't hard and rough like Grandpa's. It looks smooth and soft, like Grandma's.

I turn around. Instead of an old skeleton who has been buried for years, it's an old lady wearing a black robe and a black hood. She looks like Father Lawrence. That is, if Father Lawrence were shorter, fatter, smoother, and a woman.

"Well, are you?" she asks.

"What?" I ask, still wondering who this woman monk is.

"Michael? Are you Michael?" she asks softly.

I just nod.

"Good," she says, patting my arm. "We're going to need you to ring the bell next Christmas, too."

"We?"

She puts her arm on mine like Father Lawrence used to and walks me toward the front gate.

"Me and the twelve nuns living in the monastery," she says. "We're all too old to be swinging from that rope."

Nuns?

Women monks.

The cannibal monks of the monastery are all gone now. The younger boys in the neighborhood have nothing to worry about anymore.

Now it's the girls' turn.